HONEY BUNCH HELD UP HER HAND.

Honey Bunch: Her First Visit to the City.   *Frontispiece—(Page 86)*

HONEY BUNCH
HER FIRST VISIT TO THE CITY

BY

HELEN LOUISE THORNDYKE

AUTHOR OF "HONEY BUNCH: JUST A LITTLE
GIRL," "HONEY BUNCH: HER FIRST
DAYS ON THE FARM," ETC.

ILLUSTRATED BY
WALTER S. ROGERS

NEW YORK
GROSSET & DUNLAP
PUBLISHERS

Made in the United States of America

THE HONEY BUNCH BOOKS

BY HELEN LOUISE THORNDYKE

12mo. Cloth. Illustrated.

HONEY BUNCH: JUST A LITTLE GIRL

HONEY BUNCH: HER FIRST VISIT TO THE CITY

HONEY BUNCH: HER FIRST DAYS ON THE FARM

GROSSET & DUNLAP

Publishers : : **New York**

CONTENTS

HONEY BUNCH:
HER FIRST VISIT TO THE CITY

CHAPTER I

A BUSY LITTLE GIRL

"MOTHER," said Honey Bunch, "here's the rabbit picture."

Mrs. Morton was bending over an open trunk in her room. She turned and stared at her little girl.

"Why, Honey Bunch!" she cried, "what in the world do you expect me to do with the rabbit picture? And how did you get it down from over the table, dear?"

Honey Bunch was so little that the pretty picture of two white rabbits, in a white and gold frame, was almost as long as she was. She held on to it tightly with both hands. It was her own picture, one her daddy had given her for Christmas, and it hung in her own bedroom—or had till she had taken it down.

"I stood up on a chair," Honey Bunch explained. "Don't you want it, Mother?"

"Dearest, we can't take pictures with us," answered her mother. "There isn't going to be room in the trunk for anything we don't really need. You won't need pictures at Aunt Julia's, Honey Bunch; we'll see the most wonderful pictures in the art galleries."

Honey Bunch put the picture down on Mother's bed and stared at it.

"But, Mother," she said, "Mrs. Farriday brought all her pictures with her. She wrapped them in tissue paper and put them in her trunks. She said so. She said they wouldn't break that way."

"Oh, Honey Bunch, you must be mistaken," said Mrs. Morton. "Think, dear. I'm sure that when Mrs. Farriday went to Colorado to visit her daughter, she didn't take a single picture in her trunk."

Honey Bunch shook her head. She wanted to explain so much that the words tumbled out of her little red mouth and she stuttered—almost.

"But, Mother!" Honey Bunch cried. "Mother, I don't mean when Mrs. Farriday went to visit her little girl. I mean when they moved next door."

Mrs. Farriday, you see, lived next door to Honey Bunch. Her "little girl," as Honey Bunch called the daughter who lived in Colorado, was grown up and married and had a little girl of her own.

Honey Bunch's mother smiled a little and pulled her own little girl into her lap.

"Are you talking about the time the Farridays moved into the house next door, dear?" she asked. "Well, then, I don't doubt Mrs. Farriday brought pictures in her trunk. But we are not moving, you know, Honey Bunch; we are not going to take down our pretty curtains and pull up the rugs and move away from our house. You and I are going on a visit, to see Aunt Julia, and by and by we'll come home again. So we do not need to take anything with us except things to wear."

"Oh!" said Honey Bunch. "I—I never went visiting before, did I, Mother?"

"No, you never did," agreed her mother, kissing her. "And isn't it lovely that your very first visit is going to be to the largest American city? Why, Honey Bunch, if I had seen New York when I was a little girl like you, I don't know what I should have thought or said."

"Didn't you go to New York when you were a little girl?" asked Honey Bunch.

"No, indeed," said her mother. "I never saw New York till Daddy took me there when we were married. And now, dear, Mother has a great deal of packing to do, and she can't sit here and talk any longer. Don't you want to run upstairs and bring me those shoe-bags hanging on the door in the store-room? But first put the rabbit picture back in your room; don't stand on a chair again, though. Daddy will hang it up again to-night."

Honey Bunch slipped out of Mother's lap and trotted away, carrying the picture carefully. Upstairs she went after the shoe-bags, and on the way down she thought of an important question.

"Mother!" she said, coming back into her mother's room and handing her the shoe-bags, "could Eleanor go visiting?"

Mrs. Morton was stuffing tissue paper into a pretty dark blue blouse. She put it into the trunk and sat down in her low rocking chair before she answered.

"Honey Bunch," she said then, "do you want to take Eleanor with you very much?"

Honey Bunch sat down on the floor and thought for a moment.

"I s'pose a doll would like to see New York," she said. "And maybe she would like to ride on the train. But she is lots of trouble sometimes, Mother. Her shoes come off and I might forget her and then her feelings would be hurt."

"I wouldn't take her, if I were you," said Mrs. Morton. "A long trip really isn't very good for a doll. Then Eleanor is heavy to carry, too, and there will be so many things for you to see on the train and in the city that I'm almost sure you will sometimes find Eleanor in the way."

"But I love her," Honey Bunch said. "I love all my dolls."

"Of course you do, dear," Mrs. Morton declared. "You love Eleanor, and when you come home you will have ever so many things to tell her. I think she will be happier here with the other dolls; you couldn't carry her everywhere you go in New York, and she might be lonesome."

So Honey Bunch decided that Eleanor should stay at home. Eleanor did not seem a bit disappointed when she heard this. She smiled and smiled and when Honey Bunch put her in her crib she closed her eyes and went right to sleep and didn't wake up till Honey Bunch came home from New York. Dolls are like that, you know—they are always as good as gold.

Honey Bunch helped her mother a great deal with the packing. The trunk was a large one and when Honey Bunch first saw it she thought they would never be able to fill it up. But when Mother's pretty dresses went in and her shoes and all her pretty, frilly

things, and Honey Bunch's best petticoats and
her nicest frocks and every one of her patent
leather belts and her white kid shoes and her
socks—when all these things were in the
trunk, why, it didn't look so deep. Honey
Bunch began to think that she and Mother
might get it full to the brim, after all.

"Oh, Mother, what will Lady Clare do?"
asked Honey Bunch as she saw her mother
putting her new winter coat on a hanger.

Honey Bunch's new coat had a cunning little fur collar and it was this collar that re-
minded her of Lady Clare, the beautiful black
cat who wore an ermine collar. Lady Clare's
fur collar was not sewed on, it grew fluffily
around her throat and Honey Bunch thought
she was the nicest cat any little girl ever had.

"Didn't I tell you?" said Mrs. Morton.
"Mrs. Farriday is going to take care of Lady
Clare for us. Daddy offered to feed her, but
it isn't fair to expect him to remember all the
time. Mrs. Farriday will keep Lady Clare
in her house. She is over there so much, anyway, I think she will feel quite at home."

"Yes, I s'pect she will," Honey Bunch agreed. "She ate Mrs. Farriday's canary-bird hat, so she must think it is her house."

Alas, this was the beautiful Lady Clare's one fault. She could not see any kind of bird, even a stuffed bird on a hat, without wanting to eat it. Mrs. Farriday had had a very pretty hat with little yellow feathers on it— Honey Bunch called it a canary-bird hat, but of course Mrs. Farriday would not wear canary birds on her head—and Lady Clare had found it on the bed one day and torn it into bits. Mrs. Farriday said it was her fault for leaving the hat out of the box and she seemed just as fond of Lady Clare after that as before. Perhaps, Honey Bunch said, she liked cats better than she did hats.

Honey Bunch had been trotting up and down stairs, bringing Mother things to put in the trunk most of the afternoon, when the doorbell rang. She and Mother were on the third floor.

"I'll go, Mother!" cried Honey Bunch, who loved to answer the doorbell.

"Put this in the trunk on your way down, dear," said Mrs. Morton. "Make your head serve your heels."

Honey Bunch thought this was funny and she made a little song of it as she took the round, white package her mother gave her and ran downstairs.

"Make your head serve your heels," sang Honey Bunch. "Make your head serve your heels! Make your head serve your heels!"

She was so interested in her song that she never stopped on the second floor where the trunk was, but ran down to the front door still singing about her head and her heels.

"Oh!" said Honey Bunch, when she opened the door.

"Hello!" replied the boy who stood there. "Does Mrs. Morton live here?"

"She's Mother," answered Honey Bunch, staring at the round, white package the boy held out to her.

"Take it," he said. "It's from Gaston's bakery."

He pushed the package into Honey Bunch's

arms, on top of the other package she still held, and shut the door for her.

"What was it, Honey Bunch?" called Mother from upstairs.

"He said it was for you from the bakery," answered Honey Bunch, putting her packages down on the hall table.

"That's Daddy's birthday cake, then, but you mustn't tell him," said Mrs. Morton, leaning over the banisters. "Don't open it, dear. I want to put it away till he comes home."

"Lady Clare wants to come in, Mother," said Honey Bunch, poking her fat little finger against the cake box to see if it felt like a birthday cake. "May I let her in, Mother?"

Mrs. Morton said Lady Clare might come in, so Honey Bunch ran to the kitchen door and opened it for the cat. She was playing with her when she heard her mother calling.

"Honey Bunch, I wish you'd come up and take these magazines down to the first floor for me," called Mrs. Morton. "I want to give them away before we go."

"Oh, my, I didn't put that in the trunk!" said the little girl to herself, as she ran through the hall and saw the two packages still sitting on the table.

She took the round, white package up with her and put it carefully in an empty corner of the trunk. Then she carried down the magazines for Mother and put her clean handkerchiefs in the right box and counted her pairs of socks—Honey Bunch counted by colors, not numbers; she wasn't old enough to count numbers, but she could say, "white, blue, tan, black"—and helped her mother so much that Mrs. Morton said she didn't know what she should do without her.

"And now I'm going downstairs to get supper," said Mrs. Morton at last.

Honey Bunch was hungry after working so hard, and when she heard her mother coming upstairs again she thought she was coming to tell her to wash her face and hands and get ready for supper.

But Mrs. Morton did not say that at all. She looked worried.

"Honey Bunch," she said, "did you do anything with Daddy's birthday cake?"

"No, Mother."

"I don't see where that cake could go!" worried Mrs. Morton. "Honey Bunch, where did you put it when the boy gave it to you?"

"On the hall table, Mother," answered the little girl. "I'll show you."

CHAPTER II

THE TRAVELERS START

HONEY BUNCH ran downstairs ahead of Mother, eager to show her the cake box she had left on the hall table. But no cake box was there! Honey Bunch stared.

"I left it right there," she said. "I put it right on the table, Mother."

"And you didn't open it, dear?" asked her mother.

"No, I didn't even pull the string," said Honey Bunch earnestly. "You said not to open it, Mother, and I never touched it. Did somebody take it?"

Mrs. Morton sat down on the lowest stair step to think.

"No one could take it," she said. "No one has come to the house since the boy brought it. Oh, Honey Bunch, that was Daddy's birthday cake, and now it's gone. And I thought we could surprise him at supper!"

Honey Bunch squeezed herself in between Mother and the stair rail. She put her fluffy yellow head down on her mother's shoulder.

"Don't you care, Mother darling," she said. "Maybe we'll find it when Daddy comes; he can look on all the top shelves."

Honey Bunch's mother said she was a comfort. And she was. You may have heard of this little girl before, in the first book about her which is called "Honey Bunch: Just a Little Girl." If you have read that book you know that Honey Bunch was five years old and that her real name was Gertrude Marion Morton. Her daddy and her mother, you see, called her Honey Bunch because—well, her daddy said it was because she was so sweet he couldn't help it. Honey Bunch was a short way, he declared, of saying "bunch of sweetness." In the first book about her you will read how Honey Bunch had a tea party and what happened to the rag doll and about the pie, too. That poor pie! Honey Bunch made it and Daddy sat on it, and oh, dear, for a few minutes it looked as though there would be no pie at all.

Honey Bunch met Mr. Subways, too, in that book. And when his card was lost neither she nor Mother could remember his name. And Daddy was anxious to have them remember, but that all came out right after a bit. Then, in December, when Honey Bunch had her fifth birthday, her cousins came to visit her and it was two of these cousins, Bobby and Tess Turner, who lived in New York. Honey Bunch's "Aunt Julia" was Bobby and Tess's mother, and Honey Bunch and her mother were packing the trunk to go to see them. And that brings us back to Honey Bunch on the stairs.

"Maybe Daddy will find the cake," said Honey Bunch again.

"Oh, we must find it before he comes," said Mrs. Morton. "I wonder—Honey Bunch, I do believe I know where it is!"

Up jumped Mother and ran upstairs as fast as she could go. After her ran Honey Bunch, as fast as *she* could go. Mrs. Morton ran into

her own room and knelt down by the trunk.
She put in her arm and pulled out a round,
white package.

"Here it is!" she cried. "Isn't it lovely,
dear, we have Daddy's cake before he gets
here?"

"How did the cake get in the trunk?"
asked Honey Bunch, staring in great surprise
at the package.

"Why, dear, don't you see?" asked Mrs.
Morton. "There were two packages on the
hall table; one I gave you to put in the trunk
and the other was the cake. I suppose something took your attention for a minute, and
you took the wrong package and put it in the
trunk."

Honey Bunch nodded her yellow head.
She began to understand.

"I went out to the kitchen to let Lady Clare
in," she explained.

"Yes, that was it," said Mrs. Morton.
"And when I went downstairs to get supper,
I saw the package of collars and frills I had
given you to put in the trunk for me and I

thought you had forgotten it; so I brought it upstairs and put it in the trunk myself."

"Then was everything in the trunk?" Honey Bunch asked.

Mrs. Morton laughed. She put her arm around Honey Bunch and hugged her.

"You and I together put almost everything into the trunk," she said gaily. "And now let's go down and put the cake on the table before it gets packed again."

That cake for Honey Bunch's daddy was a beautiful cake. It was round and smooth and the icing was rich and brown with white-icing letters on the brown icing. Honey Bunch could not read what the white icing said, but Mother read it to her.

"It says, 'David Anthony Morton, January 4,'" read Mrs. Morton. "And, Honey Bunch, if you will be very careful, you may help me put the candles on."

Honey Bunch was delighted to help with the candles and she was very careful not to break the shiny icing when she stuck in the little pink rose cups that were to hold the candles.

"Daddy has lots more candles on his cake than I had," said Honey Bunch, standing back to view her work. "I guess he has a hundred."

"Why, Honey Bunch!" laughed her mother. "I'm surprised at you! Poor Daddy isn't a hundred years old! How many candles do you really think I have here for him?"

"Sixty-two," said Honey Bunch wisely.

Mrs. Morton laughed again. Then she put the last candle in its pretty cup and stood off to admire the cake.

"There are just thirty-three candles," she said. "There goes the bell! Run and let Daddy in, dear, while I light the candles."

You should have seen that beautiful cake when Honey Bunch and her daddy came into the dining-room. Thirty-three little pink candles all blazing at once looked very merry, and Daddy Morton was so delighted that he said he would have to kiss Mother thirty-three times and Honey Bunch, too.

"Blow them out and wish, Daddy," said Honey Bunch eagerly, so Daddy made his wishes and blew out his candles and then they sat down to supper.

Of course Mother and Honey Bunch had to tell him how his birthday cake was packed in the trunk by mistake and Daddy pretended to be alarmed and wondered if he ought to go upstairs and look for his favorite slippers and his best neckties.

"How do I know you haven't packed those?" he said. "I've heard that when people are getting ready to go to New York for a visit they are sometimes so excited they pack the shoes and hats they want to wear on the train."

Honey Bunch giggled, for she knew her daddy was trying to tease her. Didn't she have the prettiest new tan shoes to wear on the train and the prettiest new brown hat with a little beaver crown and a new brown coat with a beaver collar that buttoned up tight under her little round chin? Of course she did, and she didn't mean to pack them in the trunk, either. She meant to wear them.

The birthday cake was so good that Daddy had to have two pieces. He said it might be a whole year before he had any cake again. But of course he didn't mean that. Mother often baked cake and Honey Bunch helped her.

"Maybe Mother will bake you a cake at Aunt Julia's," said Honey Bunch, when she climbed into Daddy's lap after supper to kiss him good-night.

"But I shall not be there," answered Mr. Morton.

"Oh, aren't you going to New York?" asked Honey Bunch. "Does Mother know that?"

"Daddy will have to get along without cake until we come back," said Mrs. Morton, smiling a little. "He's coming to New York to bring us home. Aren't you, Daddy?"

Mr. Morton said "yes," and that made Honey Bunch feel better. She didn't know whether she would like to go visiting without her daddy but, of course, if he came after them, that would make everything all right.

The day after Mr. Morton's birthday was a busy day for Honey Bunch and her mother. Honey Bunch had to go and say good-bye to Ida Camp, who was her best friend. Ida loved Honey Bunch dearly and she said she would miss her very much while she was away.

"I'll bring you something nice, and I'll send you post cards to put in your book," Honey Bunch promised.

There were several little girls who lived on the same street as Honey Bunch, and they had all heard that she was going to New York. Honey Bunch had to say good-bye to each of them and they asked her so many questions that she couldn't answer them all.

"My cousin lives in New York," said Grace Winters. "Maybe you'll see her."

"How does she look?" asked Honey Bunch.

"Oh, she has lovely long black hair," answered Grace. "And she's in high school."

Honey Bunch didn't see why Grace should think she would meet her cousin, but then, she thought, most anything might happen in New York. Mary and Fannie Graham wanted post cards to put in their collections, and Kitty and Cora Williams asked Honey Bunch to bring them a little monkey, if she could.

"They're in the Zoo," explained Kitty. "It would be such fun to play with a monkey. Perhaps they give real little ones away."

Honey Bunch promised to bring a "real little" monkey if they did give them away at the Zoo. Then her mother called her and she had to go in, but not before Anna Martin had told her to be careful about strange dogs.

"One followed my big brother home once in New York," said Anna. "And he wouldn't go away and he wouldn't go away. He sat on the steps all night and a policeman had to come and get him in the morning!"

When Honey Bunch went into the house she found that the trunk was all packed and that Mother wanted to shampoo her hair. The expressman came for the trunk while Mrs. Morton was washing Honey Bunch's hair and the little girl had to sit very still with her head over the basin and never open her eyes once—lest soap get into them and make them smart—while Mrs. Morton went to tell the man where to get the trunk.

Bump! Bump! sounded the trunk as the expressman took it downstairs on his strong back. Bump! Bump!

"Oh, my!" whispered Honey Bunch into the soft warm towel spread under her face. "Oh, my! The trunk is going to New York and I'm going to New York and Mother's going to New York!"

And the very next day, Honey Bunch and her mother started for New York. Mr. Morton took Lady Clare over to Mrs. Farriday, who promised to take good care of her, and hardly had Honey Bunch said good-bye to Lady Clare when a green motor car rolled up to the house and Daddy hurried her and Mother down to the curb and helped them in it. In two more minutes—or so it seemed to Honey Bunch—they were at the station.

"Well, that was pretty close!" said Mr.

Morton, as he lifted Honey Bunch out and
put her on the platform. "That's the smoke
of your train now. Kiss Daddy, dear."

Honey Bunch put her arms around her
daddy's neck and hugged him so hard she
knocked her new brown hat over one ear.
Then she held tightly to his hand while he
kissed Mother, and in another moment, with
a great snorting and roaring swish, up swept
a long train and stopped just as Honey Bunch
had decided that it had forgotten where the
station was.

CHAPTER III

ON THE TRAIN

THERE was a crowd of people who wanted to get on the train, and most of them seemed to want to get on at the same time. A nice old gentleman in a blue uniform stood beside the steps of one car and he said, "Easy, easy, don't push!" But the people went right on pushing.

Suddenly the old gentleman put out his arm and held back a fat little man who carried a large suitcase and who was rushing for the steps.

"Just a minute," said the man in the blue uniform.

Then he picked up the bag Mother held and Mr. Morton took Honey Bunch in his arms and lifted her right up over all the steps at once and landed her on the platform of the car. He helped Mother up the steps next,

and then the old gentleman with the twinkly
eyes put the bag on the platform and there
Honey Bunch and Mother were, on the
train!

"Who was he?" whispered Honey Bunch,
as she followed Mother into the car.

"Here's a seat for us," said Mrs. Morton.
"See, Honey Bunch, there is Daddy on the
platform. Wave to him, dear!"

The train began to move just then and
Honey Bunch and Mother waved to Daddy
and he took off his hat and waved to them and
even ran beside the car a little way. But the
train could go much faster than he could run
and soon it was past the station and they
could not see Daddy at all.

"Who was he?" asked Honey Bunch again.
"The man with white hair, Mother, who
looked like Santa Claus?"

"That was the conductor," answered Mrs.
Morton. "You'll see him again, dear, when
he comes through the train for our tickets."

Honey Bunch had the seat next to the window, and when her mother said she had bet-

ter take off her coat she stood so that she need not miss the flying houses outside as she wriggled out of both her hat and coat. Honey Bunch wanted to see everything that was happening as the train ran all those miles to New York.

"Tickets from Barham!" called some one. "Tickets from Barham!"

"Mother, we live in Barham!" cried Honey Bunch, looking at her mother. "We live there."

"Yes, dearest; and the conductor wants our tickets," replied Mrs. Morton, opening her purse and taking out the tickets.

The white-haired conductor had a punch in his hand and he snipped a little hole in each ticket and gave them back to Honey Bunch's mother. Then he pretended to snip Honey Bunch's nose, and that made her laugh.

"Well, Miss Blue Eyes," said the conductor, smiling so that his own eyes crinkled, "aren't you afraid you will get lost in New York?"

"How did you know?" cried Honey Bunch.

"Did Mother tell you we were going to New York?"

"It's magic," said the conductor. "I know magic and that tells me where every one on this train is going."

"Fairies?" asked Honey Bunch doubtfully. "Are there fairies on the train?"

The conductor laughed and snipped the ticket the lady in the seat behind Mrs. Morton held out to him.

"Little girls are the only fairies I believe in," he said. "Your ticket told me you were going to New York. I have a little granddaughter who lives there. I should say she was about as old as you are."

"I'm five," said Honey Bunch. "Does your little granddaughter ride on the train with you?"

"Not very often," replied the conductor. "She has to stay at home and go to school, you see. She is seven years old."

Then he went on to snip more tickets, and Honey Bunch settled down to watch the towns and stations and fields she could see from the

"THANK YOU VERY MUCH," SAID THE LADY.

Honey Bunch: Her First Visit to the City.   *Page* 31

window. By and by she grew tired of staring out at the flying telegraph poles and her foot felt prickly.

"Stand in the aisle a moment, dear," said Mrs. Morton, who was reading a magazine. "Hold on to the arm of my seat and you won't fall."

Honey Bunch thought it was great fun to stand in the aisle and sway a little forward and a little back, as the train moved. She didn't want to fall down, but she didn't mind tipping a little; she liked that.

"Mother," she whispered, "look at that funny lady."

Mrs. Morton looked up, nodded, and put her finger on her lip to tell Honey Bunch she mustn't laugh. Then she went on with her reading.

Honey Bunch couldn't help looking at the lady again. She was fast asleep and her hat was tilted over her eyes. She had been knitting and her ball of wool was rolling nearer and nearer the edge of her lap.

"It'll roll off in a minute," said Honey

Bunch to herself. "I just know it will roll off."

Every time the train jerked the ball rolled almost to the edge of the lady's lap and then it rolled back again.

"Why does she go to sleep in the day time?" whispered Honey Bunch to Mother.

"She may have been traveling all night," said Mrs. Morton. "Sometimes the motion of the train makes people sleepy."

Honey Bunch looked again at the lady who was asleep. Suddenly the train tilted so much to one side that Honey Bunch thought it was going to tip over. Then it tipped back again, but not before the ball rolled out of the sleepy lady's lap and down the aisle all the way to Honey Bunch's feet.

Several people laughed, Honey Bunch stared, and the sleepy lady woke up and clutched her knitting.

"Pick it up, dear, and take it back to her," said Mrs. Morton.

Honey Bunch picked up the ball of wool— it was bright blue—and walked up the aisle, rolling up the wool as she walked. When she reached the lady who had dropped it, there it was all nicely wound up again.

"Thank you very much," said the lady, with a smile. "I won't go to sleep again." And she sat up very straight and began to knit as though she intended to keep herself wide awake.

Slowly and carefully Honey Bunch went back to where Mother sat. If you have ever walked down the aisle of a train when it is going, you know how hard it is to walk straight and not bump into people in the seats. Honey Bunch managed to do it, but she could not walk fast.

She squeezed in past her mother and then she saw a boy a few seats ahead of her. Honey Bunch saw him looking at her and she smiled. But the boy made an awful face at her and stuck out his tongue. He even got up on the seat and leaned over the back and made another face.

Honey Bunch scrambled up beside Mother and sat down. She meant to look out of the

window. But every few minutes she found
herself peeping at the boy. And every time
he made a face and each face was homelier
than the first one.

He wasn't a good-looking boy, even when
he wasn't making faces. He seemed to be
always scowling and that, you know, isn't be-
coming to any boy or girl. This boy was
short and chubby and he wore a necktie that
was always coming untied. It seemed to
Honey Bunch that his mother tied that tie for
him a dozen times. She would jerk it and
knot it and then, the moment she had finished,
the boy would look back and if he saw Honey
Bunch watching him he would make a face
at her.

The boy had a cap, too, and he was always
putting that on his head and then his mother
would take it off. Honey Bunch saw her take
it off three times and in a few moments the
boy had it back on his head.

"Honey Bunch, what are you looking at?"
asked her mother, when she saw that Honey

Bunch was not looking out of the window, but over the backs of the seats.

"There's a boy down there," answered Honey Bunch. "He's making faces at me, Mother."

Mrs. Morton looked, but the boy ducked down beside his mother and kept very still.

"I wouldn't look at him, if I were you," Mrs. Morton said. "He is trying to tease you. Some boys like to try to tease little girls. Don't let him see that you notice him at all."

"He puts his hat on and his mother takes it off," said Honey Bunch.

"He must be a bad boy if he doesn't mind his mother," Mrs. Morton told her. "Wouldn't you like to go and get Mother a drink of water, dear?"

Honey Bunch was very glad to go. She liked to do anything different and she was beginning to get the least bit tired of the train. She had not thought that New York could be so far away.

"Take this paper cup and be careful not to

fill it too full. Then you won't spill it," said
Mrs. Morton. "You can't reach the cups by
the cooler. I know they are out of your
reach."

Honey Bunch felt very important as she
started out. She knew where the water was
for she had watched people going to get a
drink. But when she reached the shiny faucet
and the little brass mat where you stood while
you filled your cup, there was that bad boy
ahead of her!

"Hello!" he said. "What do you want?"

"A drink of water for Mother," replied
Honey Bunch, holding out her paper cup.

She thought the boy would fill it for her.
She was used to having people help her and
be nice to her.

"You'll have to wait," said the boy, acting
as though he did not see her cup. "I was
here first and you'll just have to wait."

So Honey Bunch waited politely. The
boy had a glass in his hand and he filled it,
then emptied the water out and filled the glass
again. He let the glass brim over and

emptied it the second time. Honey Bunch wondered if he would ever be through.

He was letting the water run slowly into the glass again when the car door slammed. A brakeman came into the car.

"Now you kids want to quit playing in that water," he said gruffly. "That's good ice water and you mustn't waste it."

He went on down the car and never even noticed that poor Honey Bunch had no water in her cup. He thought she was playing with the boy.

"I guess it's cold enough now," said the boy, sticking out his tongue at Honey Bunch and shutting off the faucet.

His glass was so full that it dripped as he took it out. Honey Bunch stepped up to the little brass mat and the boy brushed against her. Down trickled the water from his glass, splashed against her sleeve, soaking the white pique to the little arm underneath, and on down, making ugly stains on the new tan shoes Honey Bunch wore.

"There now, see what you've done!" ex-

claimed the boy, just as if Honey Bunch was
to blame.

"Oh, my!" sighed Honey Bunch sadly,
standing on tiptoe to reach the shiny faucet.
"What a bad boy you are!"

She managed to fill her cup and went back
to find her mother waiting for her a bit anx-
iously.

CHAPTER IV

THE BAD BOY

"WHAT kept you so long, dear?" asked Mrs. Morton. "Your sleeve is soaking wet! Did you have trouble, Honey Bunch?"

The water cooler was at the other end of the car, behind Mrs. Morton's seat, and she could not see it from where she sat.

"That bad boy who made faces at me, splashed me, Mother," said Honey Bunch indignantly. "I wish I'd splashed him back!"

"Oh, that wouldn't be the thing to do at all," Mrs. Morton declared, trying to dry the wet sleeve with her handkerchief. "If you did that I should be mortified! You wouldn't want to make your mother feel ashamed of you, would you, dear?"

"No-o," said Honey Bunch. "Is that boy's mother ashamed of him, Mother?"

"I'm afraid she must be," replied Mrs.

37

Morton, giving Honey Bunch a kiss. "Thank you for the water, dear. And now I'll read you a story, if you'll curl up here beside me and listen."

Honey Bunch put her head in Mother's lap to listen, and before the story was half finished she was asleep. When she woke Mother told her that in another half hour they would be in New York.

The first thing Honey Bunch thought of when she felt real wide awake and was sitting up straight, ready to watch for New York from the windows, was the boy who made faces at her. She peeped down the aisle. He wasn't there.

"Perhaps he got off at the station where we were when I woke up," said Honey Bunch to herself. "Yes, I guess he did. I wonder if he makes faces all the time!"

Then, to amuse herself, Honey Bunch breathed on the window and drew pictures with her finger. She drew a picture of Lady Clare and a picture of Aunt Julia and pictures of Bobby and Tess. Almost as fast as she drew them they faded, but it was easy to breathe again on the window and draw more.

The white-haired conductor came through the car again just as Honey Bunch had finished a whole batch of pictures.

"Do you like to draw?" he asked her, smiling.

"Pictures, I do," said Honey Bunch. "At home I have colored crayons."

"I think I have a picture in my pocket that my little granddaughter drew and sent to me," said the conductor. "I'll show it to you."

He felt in his inside coat pocket and drew out a flat pocketbook, like the kind Honey Bunch's daddy carried in his pocket. There were a great many papers in the conductor's pocketbook, but he seemed to think that the most important one was a little sheet of yellow paper folded in the middle. He took this out carefully and opened it.

"There!" he said. "That's a picture of a pansy she drew in school."

"Why, that's a lovely picture!" cried Honey

Bunch. "I like black and yellow pansies. We have them in our yard, don't we, Mother?"

"Yes, indeed," said Mrs. Morton, folding the paper up and handing it back to the conductor. "Haven't you a picture of your little grandchild with you?" she asked him.

He nodded and smiled and put the paper back in its place. Then he turned the pocketbook around and opened another place. He drew out a piece of brown cardboard.

"Here she is," he said proudly.

Honey Bunch climbed up on the seat and kneeled down to look over Mother's shoulder. They saw the picture of a merry-eyed little girl with two long braids of hair wrapped around her head and fastened with a bow over each ear. She was smiling at them and Honey Bunch smiled, too, when she saw her.

"What is her name?" said Honey Bunch to the conductor.

"Her name is Mary," he said. "I've always said she was the sweetest little girl in New

York, but after you get there I'll have to say she is one of the two sweetest."

He put the picture back in his pocketbook and went away.

"I like Mary's grandpa, don't you, Mother?" said Honey Bunch. "And I like Mary. Maybe we'll see her in New York."

"Oh, no, dear, not in New York," answered Mrs. Morton quickly. "In that big city there are a thousand and one little girls named Mary. In Barham you might meet Mary because it is a much smaller place, but in New York even if you did see her you wouldn't know her."

Honey Bunch was thinking about Mary and wondering if she liked to live in New York when she looked down the aisle and there was the bad boy! He had not left the train at all, but he had had a long nap, though Honey Bunch did not know this, of course. He had been asleep with his head on his mother's shoulder and so Honey Bunch could not see him over the backs of the seats.

He made a face at her as soon as he saw

her. His mother was still asleep and he
thought this was a good chance for him to
put on his cap. It was a black and white
cap and the boy seemed to like it very much.
He pulled it on and then pulled at his necktie
till it hung in a string. In fact he did everything his mother had told him not to do.

"Mother," whispered Honey Bunch, "he's
going to open the window. Shall I open
ours?"

"No, indeed," replied Mrs. Morton. "It is
too cold a day. You see those little narrow
windows up there near the roof of the car?
They are the ventilators and the conductor
and brakeman open and close them to give
us all the fresh air we need. I think that
boy is very naughty to open the window while
his mother is asleep."

"I think he is, too," agreed Honey Bunch.
"Bobby told me his mother puts him in the
closet when he is bad. Maybe that boy's
mother will put him in the closet."

The boy worked at the window some time
before he could raise it. There were two

catches to press and the window was heavy and, as it had not been opened every day, it stuck when he tried to lift it. Then, suddenly, it went up with a bang.

"Here, what are you doing?" cried the boy's mother, sitting up with a jerk. The noise had wakened her.

She wore a tall feather in her hat and the strong wind from the open window bent it down so that it was blown into her eyes. She did not like it at all. And indeed the January breeze can sting like little sharp icicles.

"Shut that window at once, Lester!" Honey Bunch heard her say to the bad boy. "What do you mean by opening it? The idea!"

"Aw, Ma, leave it up a little while," said Lester. "I'm too hot, Ma. A little cold air won't hurt any one."

"The idea!" said his mother again. "You can't have any sense at all. Opening a car window in the dead of winter! Put it down at once! Do you hear me?"

The bad boy looked as though he was going to say something else, but his mother stood up and said "Lester!" again very loudly and tried to push him out of the way so that she could pull down the window.

"Oh, I'll shut it!" he said crossly. "I guess you'll be sorry when I get sick from staying in this stuffy old car. Leave me alone, Ma! I'm shutting it! Can't you see I am?"

The window was just as hard to pull down as it had been to put up. The bad boy fussed with the catches and jumped up and down and tried to rattle it and poke it. The car was growing colder and several people began to look over to the open window and to grumble that they didn't mean to freeze to death.

"I've got it now!" cried the boy. But just as he said that, pouf! a stronger blast of wind than ever blew in and lifted his cap from his head. He tried to catch it, but missed it. Away sailed the black and white cap out of the window!

"Now I hope you're satisfied! See what you've done!" And almost before Honey Bunch knew what she meant to do, the bad boy's mother stood up and smacked the boy on one cheek and shut down the window with such a crash that it made the other windows in the car rattle.

"Don't you let me hear a word from you the rest of this trip!" scolded the bad boy's mother, sitting down again.

And goodness, no one heard another word from that boy. He didn't make another face at Honey Bunch. He didn't go out into the aisle. He sat quietly in his seat and looked out of the window.

"Time to put on your hat and coat now, dear," said Mrs. Morton, in a few moments.

"Look at the walls!" cried Honey Bunch, as she was being buttoned into her coat. "Look, Mother!"

Their train was now running between two high gray walls and there were no fields or trees or houses or towns to be seen.

"We're almost in the Terminal," explained Mrs. Morton.

"Is the Terminal New York?" asked Honey Bunch, as her mother put her hat on.

"It's the large station where the tracks end

and the trains stop," said Mrs. Morton. "I hope Aunt Julia will be able to come and meet us."

All around them people were putting on their hats and coats and taking down the satchels from the little wire baskets where they kept them during the trip.

"Oh, oh! It's dark, Mother!" cried Honey Bunch excitedly.

It *was* dark, for the train had pulled into the long shed that was the roof over the tracks. Mrs. Morton told Honey Bunch this and then said that they would wait quietly a few moments and let those who were in a hurry go first.

"Here you are!" said the conductor, lifting Honey Bunch to the platform, when she and Mother finally went out of the car. "Good-bye, and I hope you'll enjoy your visit."

"Good-bye," called Honey Bunch, clinging to Mother with one hand and waving the other. "Tell Mary I liked the picture of her pansy!"

Mrs. Morton and Honey Bunch hurried up

the long platform that seemed to have no
end. Every one else was hurrying too. When
they passed through an iron gate into a beautiful large room built all of marble, there
were more crowds of people in a still greater
hurry.

"Look at the people tied in!" said Honey
Bunch, looking at a group who stood behind
a heavy rope stretched between two rings.

"There's Aunt Julia!" cried Mrs. Morton.

A tall lady came around from behind the
rope and walked up to them. She kissed Mrs.
Morton and then she kissed Honey Bunch.

"Well, sweetheart!" she said, lifting the little girl off her feet as she hugged her. "So
here you are at last in New York!"

CHAPTER V

HONEY BUNCH IN NEW YORK

HONEY BUNCH had never seen so many people in her life or such a large building. There were tall iron gates and marble walls and *such* a slippery marble floor to walk on and a great bronze clock and the most fascinating round place with different windows and a crowd at every window.

"That's where you find out which train to take," said Aunt Julia, when she saw Honey Bunch looking at the people.

There didn't seem to be any end to that Terminal. They walked from one marble room to another and still they didn't come to the street. In the station at Barham, Honey Bunch knew that if you went in one door and out another on the other side of the station, you had seen the whole place.

"I must send Daddy a telegram to tell him we are here safely," said Honey Bunch's mother.

So over to a telegraph window they went, and while Mother wrote her message Honey Bunch watched the people all about her. There was a woman with two large satchels and five little children; they were going somewhere, surely. There was a young man with a tall dog fastened to a leather strap; they seemed to be waiting for some one. There were two little girls about as old as Honey Bunch, sitting in one of the seats and talking to a boy who carried a suitcase nearly as large as he was.

"Why, there's Mother!" said Honey Bunch in surprise, looking at a lady walking away from her.

It would never do to have Mother forget her little girl in this great place, so Honey Bunch began to run. She ran after the lady in the blue coat and had almost reached her when she heard some one calling.

"Honey Bunch! Honey Bunch! Come

back here, dear!" the some one called to her.

Honey Bunch turned around and there stood her own mother!

"Why!" said Honey Bunch. "Why! Why, Mother!"

Then she ran back and slipped her hand into Mother's.

"I thought that was you," said Honey Bunch, faintly.

"I wouldn't go off and forget my little girl," said Mrs. Morton smilingly. "Now the telegram has gone to tell Daddy that we are here all right and all we have to think of is how to reach Aunt Julia's house."

"And that is what Aunt Julia is here for," declared that lady, pinching Honey Bunch's cheek. "I think, Edith, we'll take a bus and walk over."

Honey Bunch held fast to Mother's hand as they came out into the street. She thought every one in the station must have walked out with them, but if she had looked back she would have seen just as many people inside the station as ever. The trains kept bringing them in and taking them away and there would always be a crowd.

Honey Bunch and Mother and Aunt Julia had to wait for a few minutes before they could cross the street. A few people dashed ahead and wriggled between the automobiles and slid under the horses' noses, but that was really not safe, and Honey Bunch was glad Aunt Julia did not ask her to run.

"Look at all the automobiles!" she cried. "Look at the green one, Mother! See the little dog!"

There was a small black dog sitting in the big green automobile which drove slowly past and he wagged his tail when he saw Honey Bunch.

"He must like little girls," said Honey Bunch, but just then a whistle blew and Mother hurried her across the street.

All the automobiles were going the other way now and Honey Bunch wondered how people in New York ever kept from being run over. She was mighty glad when they had reached the other side of the street. But how cold she was! A wind swept down the street and blew into her face so hard that it brought the tears into her eyes.

"Wait a minute," said Aunt Julia. "I don't believe Honey Bunch can breathe in this wind."

Well, just for a minute, Honey Bunch thought so, too. That was the coldest wind she had ever known. She hid her face against Mother's coat.

"It's these tall buildings," she heard Aunt Julia say. "We'll take the bus in a moment, dear, and then you'll be all right."

They walked on presently, and came to another street, a wide street and filled with automobiles, of course. It seemed to Honey Bunch that all the automobiles in the world must be in New York. She and Mother and Aunt Julia stood on the corner and Honey Bunch, looking down the avenue, saw a wide, comfortable looking automobile lumbering easily toward them.

"What a fat automobile!" said Honey Bunch.

It was a fat automobile and Honey Bunch liked the way it looked—as though it would hold a good many people and not squeeze them. To her delight, Aunt Julia held up her hand and the automobile stopped.

There was a conductor on the platform and he helped Honey Bunch up the step. She was going to climb up the iron stairs that wound around in back of him but Aunt Julia said to go inside.

Inside the car were comfortable seats, and Honey Bunch found a place by the window. Mother sat beside her and Aunt Julia sat in the seat ahead.

"Where do the stairs go?" asked Honey Bunch eagerly.

She meant the winding iron stairs, and Aunt Julia explained that they went up to the roof of the bus.

"There are seats up there, too," she said. "In summer it is very pleasant to ride outside, but on a day like this the wind would blow you right off into the river, I'm afraid."

Honey Bunch was sure that she would not like to ride on the roof on such a cold day. The people she saw through the window were hurrying along as though they were cold. The men had their hands in their pockets and the collars of their coats turned up and the ladies were almost hidden under their furs.

"Well, Honey Bunch," smiled Aunt Julia, as the bus stopped to take on more passengers, "how do you think you are going to like New York?"

"I like it," said Honey Bunch. "I like to ride in the bus. When shall we see Bobby and Tess?"

"Just the minute we reach home," replied Aunt Julia. "They would have liked to come down to the station with me, but they go to school, you know. Now two more blocks and we come to our street."

Honey Bunch was watching a little girl across the aisle push her dime into the little box the conductor held out for it—every time any one put in a dime Honey Bunch expected a Jack-in-the-box to pop out, but he never did—when Aunt Julia said:

"Here's our corner."

The bus stopped and the conductor swung Honey Bunch from the platform to the curb. Mother took one hand and Aunt Julia the other and away they went again. Honey Bunch thought it was fun to hurry, and her cheeks were as red as poppies when they came to a wide gray stone building with four little green trees set in tubs outside the door.

"Christmas trees!" said Honey Bunch wisely.

Inside the building was a boy in a blue suit with brass buttons who smiled at Aunt Julia. He was a colored boy and seemed very good-natured.

"Have the children come home yet, Dorry?" asked Aunt Julia.

"Yas'm, they're home," replied Dorry.

There was a black and gold elevator in the hall and Aunt Julia led her guests to this. Honey Bunch liked the "feel" of walking over the red velvet carpet and she thought the elevator was very beautiful. There was a mirror in it and she could see herself from the top of her hat to her tan shoes.

Dorry came to run the elevator and Honey Bunch was sure she could make it go herself as she watched him. All he did was to slide a bar down and pull it up and she thought that couldn't be very hard.

"You would like to do it, little miss?" said Dorry suddenly.

Honey Bunch jumped. She was surprised.

"Yes, I could, couldn't I?" she said eagerly.

Dorry stopped the elevator carefully before an iron gate and opened the door.

"Maybe, when you're bigger," he said seriously. "Elevators is good things for children to let alone."

There were three doors in the hall facing them. A pink-shaded light burned pleasantly and at the end of the hall Honey Bunch saw two windows. Dorry shut the elevator gate and down went the car, slowly and carefully.

"How do you know which door is yours?" asked Honey Bunch.

"They do look alike, don't they?" said Aunt
Julia, with a smile. "But, of course, we
know our own door. There—that's one way
to tell, Honey Bunch!"

The center door had been jerked open as
she was speaking and out rushed Bobby and
Tess. They pounced upon Honey Bunch and
her mother and pulled them in.

"We're so glad you're here!" they cried.
"Isn't it fun? Can we take Honey Bunch to
dancing school with us, Aunt Edith? Did
you ride in the subway yet? Isn't it cold out?
Did Dorry tell you, Mother, that the window catch is fixed?"

"Children, children," said Aunt Julia.
"Wait a moment! Here is poor tired little
Honey Bunch, hungry and cold, and you
haven't even asked her to take off her hat.
Can't you stop talking long enough to let
Honey Bunch and Aunt Edith get rested?"

Well, of course, Bobby and Tess didn't
want to be impolite, so they both rushed at
Honey Bunch and tried to take off her hat
and coat for her. Bobby pulled off her hat

and Tess nearly pulled her coat collar off,
trying to unhook it.

"Let me do it," said Honey Bunch's mother,
and in a few minutes Honey Bunch had her
coat and hat off and was ready for the late
lunch the maid brought them. Every one
else had had lunch, but Aunt Julia said she
knew Honey Bunch and her mother would
be hungry traveling, and they were.

"What shall we do now?" said Tess, when
Honey Bunch had eaten the last mouthful of
her baked apple. "There's time to go out
and play before Daddy comes home."

"I know what one little girl is going to do,"
said Honey Bunch's mother, smiling.

"Oh, what?" asked Tess, and Honey Bunch
looked interested, too.

"Have a nice nap," answered Mrs. Morton, "and be all ready for a happy day to-
morrow in New York."

"I don't need a nap, Mother," said Honey
Bunch. "I did go to sleep on the train."

"Well, suppose you let Mother brush your

hair and change your dress," said Mrs. Morton. "Then we'll see how you feel."

Aunt Julia took them into the pretty bedroom which was waiting for them, she said, and then left them alone. And Mrs. Morton had not finished unbuttoning all the buttons on Honey Bunch's frock before that small girl was sound asleep, right in her mother's lap. Mothers, you see, can tell when naps are needed. Honey Bunch's mother could.

CHAPTER VI

GOING TO MARKET

THE next day Honey Bunch was wide awake and dressed and out in the living room before any one else.

"Stay right there, dear, till I come," said Mrs. Morton, who was brushing her own hair. "Don't go into any other room, because we're up early and you might disturb some one."

Honey Bunch trotted out into the large, square room and found that some one else was up. This some one was the maid, in her blue dress and white apron.

"Good morning," she said, smiling. "You're up early."

"I woke up," said Honey Bunch. "Do you live in New York?"

"Yes, I do—always have," said the maid, picking up some tiny scraps of paper and

60

throwing them in the fireplace. "You come from Barham, don't you? Miss Tess and Master Bobby told me you are their cousin."

"I'm Honey Bunch," said the little girl. "What is your name?"

"I'm Teresa," the maid answered. "Now, Miss Honey Bunch, if I light this fire, will you promise to stand back, away from the fire screen?"

"Of course she will, Teresa," said a hearty voice. "I'll watch the fire. Hello there, Honey Bunch, what do you think of New York?"

Honey Bunch knew that the smiling-faced, twinkling-eyed gentleman holding out both hands to her must be Uncle Paul, Bobby and Tess's daddy. Honey Bunch had never seen him before, though Aunt Julia had visited them in Barham several times. Teresa put a match to the neat fire she had laid on the hearth and the crackling flames shot up the chimney.

"You must be an early riser," said Uncle Paul, giving Honey Bunch a kiss. "Tess has just opened one eye and Bobby hasn't his shoes on yet. All right, Teresa, I'll look after it."

Teresa emptied the brass coal scuttle filled with coal on the fire and went away. Uncle Paul sat down before the fire and patted the broad arm of his chair.

"Suppose you come and sit here and we'll get acquainted," he said.

Honey Bunch scrambled up beside him and he put an arm around her and they began to talk. Honey Bunch told him all about Lady Clare and how she was going to stay with Mrs. Farriday till her little mistress came home. She told Uncle Paul about her doll, Eleanor, and about Daddy and how much she loved him. She told him about the bad boy on the train who had made faces at her.

"Bobby wouldn't do that, would he, Uncle Paul?" said Honey Bunch.

"I hope not," answered Uncle Paul.

"Wouldn't do what?" cried Bobby, bursting into the room like a small cyclone. "Oh, Daddy, how long have you been here?"

"Long enough to get acquainted with Honey Bunch," replied his daddy. "And long enough to hear about a bad boy who made faces on the train, Bobby."

"Well, I don't make faces—much," said Bobby comfortably. "Here's Aunt Edith!"

Mrs. Morton and Bobby's mother came in together and Tess dashed through the door a few minutes later. Tess was in such a hurry to see her aunt and cousin that her hair-ribbon wasn't tied and one of her shoes was not laced.

"You can't come to the breakfast table like that, Tess," said her mother firmly. "Go back and finish dressing, dear."

Tess looked as though she would much rather stay where she was, but she went back to her room and when Teresa came to say that breakfast was ready, Tess came in with her hair-ribbon nicely tied and both shoes laced. Honey Bunch thought she looked much better.

"Daddy," said Bobby, as they sat down at the table, "can't we stay home from school while Honey Bunch is here? She doesn't have to go to school, and I think it's mean if we have to go all the time."

"Yes, Daddy," said Tess earnestly, "couldn't we stay home?"

"Certainly not," said Mr. Turner. "How would you ever be able to pass this June? Honey Bunch, when she starts school, will have to go every day. She won't be able to stay at home when you go to visit her."

"But we won't go, only in vacation," argued Bobby.

"Oh, well, I suppose we can play in the afternoons," said Tess. "We get home at two o'clock, and then we can play with Honey Bunch. Only I do hate to miss such a lot of fun."

"Never mind, Tess," said Honey Bunch's mother. "You might get tired going around with us. All the things that are old to you will be new to us, you know, and it isn't much fun seeing the old things over and over."

Still when Mrs. Turner said that Bobby and Tess must start for school, if they were not to be late, both children said they didn't see what any one ever invented school for!

"Oh, my, don't tell me I have two Grumbles in my family!" cried Mr. Turner, pretending to be frightened. "Mother, we haven't two Grumbles in the house, have we?"

"What's a Grumble?" asked Honey Bunch.

"A Grumble is a girl or a boy who doesn't like anything," explained her uncle. "He or she doesn't like the weather or school or what there is for breakfast. There is nothing I dislike more than a Grumble."

"I'm not a Grumble!" shouted Bobby.

"Neither am I!" cried Tess.

"Perhaps I've made a mistake," said Mr. Turner. "Honey Bunch, does Tess look like a Grumble to you?"

"No, she doesn't," said Honey Bunch quickly.

"Well, what about Bobby?" asked Mr. Turner. "Does he look like a Grumble to you?"

"Oh, no," said kind little Honey Bunch.

"He doesn't look like a Grumble, Uncle Paul."

"All right then, that's fine," said her uncle. "I always dread a day if the Grumbles start it."

Tess and Bobby kissed every one good-bye—right around the table—and started off to school looking much more contented. Perhaps the thought that their daddy was afraid they were Grumbles frightened them, too.

"Run to the window, Honey Bunch, and you can wave to them," said Mrs. Turner.

Honey Bunch ran to the dining-room window—the apartment house was on a corner—and looked down into the street. She could see Tess's red coat and Bobby's plaid cap far down in the street.

"I'll lift you up," said her uncle, and he raised the window and held Honey Bunch tightly while she waved her handkerchief to Tess and Bobby.

Then Uncle Paul had to go to the office and Aunt Julia said she must go to market.

"I wonder if Honey Bunch would like to go with me?" said her aunt.

Now, of course, Honey Bunch would like to go and she said so. Mrs. Morton said she would rather stay at home and write a letter to Honey Bunch's daddy.

"What shall I say to Daddy for you, Honey Bunch?" she asked.

"Tell him I'm going to market with Aunt Julia and that I love him very much," said Honey Bunch, and Mother promised to put that in her letter.

"Good morning," said Dorry, when Honey Bunch and her aunt stepped into the elevator.

Aunt Julia had told Honey Bunch she might ring the bell that brought the elevator up. Honey Bunch thought it was much more exciting to ride than to walk downstairs.

"Good morning," said Honey Bunch to Dorry. "We're going to market."

"Don't let the crabs bite you," answered Dorry, showing all his white teeth in a smile.

Out in the street Honey Bunch pranced along beside Aunt Julia. There were no yards to be seen anywhere, just rows and rows of houses. The sun was not shining and it was cold, though the wind did not blow.

"Where is the market?" asked Honey Bunch. "Sometimes my mother takes a basket when we go to market and I help her bring things home."

"Well, you see, dear," said Aunt Julia, "I don't go to any one market. There are many small stores on the street where we are going and I look at the food and have them send what I buy."

"Will the crabs bite me?" asked Honey Bunch, remembering what Dorry had said.

Aunt Julia laughed as she looked up and down for automobiles before crossing the street.

"I think Dorry was teasing you," she said, taking Honey Bunch's hand and running across the car tracks as fast as Tess could have run.

While her aunt was marketing, Honey Bunch watched the people. There were no car tracks on the street where Tess and Bobby

lived, but here, where the stores were, they
had trolley cars and automobiles and busses
and—baby carriages. Honey Bunch liked
the baby carriages very much. She tried to
peep under the hoods and now and then she
saw a nice, round, fat baby fast asleep on a
pillow.

On one corner they saw a man playing a
banjo and a little dog holding out a tin cup.

"Look at the dog!" cried Honey Bunch.
"Look, Aunt Julia, he can stand on his hind
legs."

"He wants you to put a penny in his cup,"
said Aunt Julia. "Go and drop these in the
cup for him, dear."

Honey Bunch went up to the little dog and
dropped the five pennies her aunt had given
her one by one into the cup the dog held.
Every time he heard a penny drop, he barked,
and Honey Bunch wanted to hug him. But
before she could even pat him, the man with
the banjo began to sing and Honey Bunch
turned and ran.

"Why, dear, what is the matter?" asked

Aunt Julia. "Did the dog frighten you?"

There was a girl standing on the pavement, shoving a baby carriage back and forth. She laughed.

"I guess the singing scared her," she said.

Honey Bunch did not say anything. The singing *had* frightened her, but she did not think it would be polite to say so.

"He thinks he sings almost nice, I s'spect," she told her mother that night. "It would hurt his feelings if I said I ran because I didn't know he meant to sing."

When Honey Bunch and Aunt Julia were through buying good things to eat, they went home. Honey Bunch didn't see how her aunt knew the way home, for they had turned several corners and crossed different streets, but Aunt Julia said no one could lose her in her own city.

Bobby and Tess had lunch at their school, but they came bouncing in at two o'clock and when they asked if they could take Honey Bunch out to play, the two mothers said "yes."

"I think it will snow before night," said
Aunt Julia, sitting down comfortably with
her knitting by the fire, which was now a
lovely bed of green and blue coals.

"Don't stay out too long," said Honey
Bunch's mother, who sat in a big chair on the
other side of the fire.

CHAPTER VII

ROCKET'S RAG DOLL

"I WISH——" said Tess, as they were going down in the elevator, "I wish that I had roller skates!"

"So do I," said Bobby.

"So do I," said Honey Bunch, though she had never thought of roller skates till that minute.

"The day you-all gets roller skates," said Dorry, opening the gate for them, "I leaves."

Tess only laughed and jumped down the three stone steps in one jump. Honey Bunch could only hop one step at a time, but Bobby and Tess were eight years old and Honey Bunch was just five.

Bobby and Tess were twins, you see, and what one didn't think of to do, the other did. That was what their daddy said. To-day

Bobby suggested that they go and see Kenneth Evans.

"Oh, no," cried Tess. "Let's take Honey Bunch to see Maudie Gray. She has a see-saw in her yard and that's lots of fun."

"But Kenneth has a dog," said Bobby. "His name is Rocket, Honey Bunch, and we have fun playing with him."

Honey Bunch looked anxious. She remembered how Bobby had pulled off her hat and Tess had nearly pulled out her coat sleeve. She was afraid Bobby might try to take her to see Kenneth Evans' dog and Tess try to take her to the girl with the seesaw at the same time. Honey Bunch knew that the twins did not always agree.

"All right, let's go and see Kenneth," said Tess suddenly. "Last time I fell off Maudie's seesaw I hurt my elbow."

Honey Bunch was glad that Tess had decided to do as Bobby wanted to. She walked between the twins and was so happy that she hummed a little song.

Kenneth Evans lived on the next block,

Bobby said, and as soon as they had turned the corner and crossed a street, Honey Bunch saw the dog.

"Why, he's just like Teddy!" she cried. "Tess, he's just like the dog Grace Winters has at home."

Kenneth was sitting on his front steps and there were several girls and boys with him. He was a freckled-faced boy with merry eyes and when Bobby said, "this is my cousin, Honey Bunch," Kenneth pulled off his cap and put out his hand.

"Hello," he said. "You going to live here?"

"No, she's visiting us," said Tess. "Does Rocket know any new tricks, Kenneth?"

Rocket, the dog, did look like the Teddy who belonged to Grace Winters. Teddy was the bad little dog that had run off with the rag doll at Honey Bunch's tea party, and it wasn't likely that she would forget him. Rocket was brown and white, like Teddy, but he had much better manners.

"Shake hands, Rocket," said Kenneth, and

Rocket held up a white paw for Honey Bunch to shake.

"Make him do it to me, Kenneth!" cried Tess, and Rocket obligingly shook hands with all the boys and girls.

Then Honey Bunch told them about Teddy and how he had treated the rag doll, and Kenneth wanted Laura Bennett, one of the little girls, to lend him her rag doll right away.

"I want to see if Rocket will run away with it," said Kenneth.

"He won't run away with my rag doll," said Laura hastily, "because I won't let him touch it."

"He won't hurt a rag doll," urged Tess, who didn't care much for dolls.

"Yes, he would," said Honey Bunch. "Don't let him have your doll. I guess rag dolls have feelings, same as other dolls."

But Kenneth was interested in the story of Teddy, and as he was a determined small boy he soon thought of a way to get a doll.

"I'll make one," he said. "Lend me your

handkerchiefs, and I'll make a rag doll. Then we'll see what Rocket will do."

Honey Bunch had a gay little pink lawn handkerchief, a new one, and Tess and Laura had blue ones. Carol Mason, another little girl, had no handkerchief, for she had lost it in school that morning, but she took off her black silk middy tie and Kenneth said that was better than a handkerchief. He liked it so much that Tess gave him her red silk tie and the boys—Bobby and Harold Brown and Dick Alverson and Kenneth—all took off their neckties and Kenneth used them and their handkerchiefs, too.

"Now I guess that looks like a doll!" he said, when he had knotted and tied all these things together. "Look, Rocket! Want to play catch?"

The ties and handkerchiefs did make a fat bundle, and it looked like a rag doll except that it didn't have any face or arms or legs.

"But Rocket won't know the difference," said Kenneth, when Tess told him this.

Rocket wasn't at all fussy about the kind

of plaything he had. The moment Kenneth let him take the doll in his mouth he began to toss it up in the air and let it fall. Kenneth threw it a little way up the street and Rocket ran after it and brought it back.

"Why doesn't he take it and run and let us chase him?" asked Tess. She liked to run and she could run fast.

"I'll tie it on a string and then we'll run and let him chase it," said Kenneth, patting Rocket, whose red tongue hung out as he panted after his last dash.

So Kenneth tied the rag doll he had made to a piece of string—which he had in his pocket—and then, dragging the doll after him, started to run up the street, Rocket and the children after him.

"Run faster!" cried Tess to Honey Bunch. "Come on, run faster; they'll all get ahead of us!"

Honey Bunch was running as fast as she could. She looked back over her shoulder to see if Rocket had grabbed the rag doll and then she saw something that made her stop and stare.

A boy put out his foot and stepped on the string. The string broke, he picked up the little bundle of ties and handkerchiefs, dirty now from dragging in the dust, and away he ran, around the corner, as fast as his feet could carry him. That was pretty fast, too, because he was a large boy, taller than Kenneth or Bobby or even Harold Brown, who was eleven.

"Bobby!" cried Honey Bunch. "Oh, Bobby! Come back here!"

The children came running back, Kenneth still trailing the broken string.

"A boy took the rag doll!" cried Honey Bunch. "He ran off with it! There, around the corner!"

"I thought Rocket grabbed it," said Kenneth. "Come on, let's chase the fellow who took it."

But though they ran around the corner and down two blocks, not a sign of the boy could they see.

"It's four o'clock and I have to go in," said
Kenneth, when they had walked slowly back
to his house. "I'm sorry about the handkerchiefs. Mine was new Christmas."

All the middy ties were new, too, and some
of the children didn't feel exactly comfortable about losing them.

"Where is your tie, Bobby?" asked Mrs.
Turner, as soon as she saw her little son.

Bobby told what had happened and his
mother looked as though she didn't know
whether to laugh or scold.

"Next time, don't take off anything," she
said. "I remember the day you and Tess
used your brand-new rubbers for ships and
let them sail down the sewer. I wish,
lambies, that after this you would try to remember not to take off anything you may
have on—gloves, overshoes or ties—without
first asking Mother. Can you remember
that?"

The twins said they thought they could and
then Mrs. Turner found a pink handkerchief
in her handkerchief box which she insisted

on giving to Honey Bunch because she had
lost hers.

"But if I hadn't told Kenneth about Teddy,
he wouldn't have made the rag doll," said
Honey Bunch. "I did it, Aunt Julia."

"You mean you think you put the idea in
Kenneth's head?" said her aunt. "Well, dear,
I don't see that you are to blame at all. When
you know Kenneth Evans as long as I have,
you'll know that he doesn't keep out of mischief or let his friends stay out very long."

"It's snowing!" cried Bobby, who didn't
want his mother to talk any more about lost
ties and handkerchiefs. "Oh, gee, it's really
snowing!"

The three children rushed to the windows.
Sure enough, beautiful little feathery flakes
were beginning to whirl softly through the
air. Some landed on the stone window sill
and lay there a moment, then melted away
and left little wet spots. Honey Bunch
wished they would last longer.

"Let us go out, Mother?" begged Bobby
and Tess. "Just a little while, Mother? We

won't stay out long. Honey Bunch never saw it snow in New York! Did you, Honey Bunch?"

Honey Bunch shook her head. No, she said, but she had seen it snow in Barham.

"And snow is snow, whether in New York or Barham," said Mrs. Turner, smiling. "I want Tess to practice her half hour now, and, Bobby, you think of something nice to do to please Honey Bunch."

Tess had begun to take music lessons and she was very proud of the book filled with skippy little black notes. She couldn't read many of them yet, but some day she would know the whole book. She washed her hands and climbed up on the piano bench while Bobby went off to get his paper soldiers to show Honey Bunch.

They were playing soldiers together when Mr. Turner came in and his overcoat was flecked with snow. He said that he thought the snow would last all night and that there might be some left over in the morning.

"If too many children don't go out and

scuffle in it to-night," he said, his kind eyes twinkling across the dinner table at Bobby.

Bobby, who had been teasing his mother to let him go out and play, "just a little," in the snow, laughed good-naturedly.

"What isn't scuffled off, the street cleaners will cart away," he answered.

"Not in the park along Riverside Drive," said his daddy. "You can go over there."

"I wish there would be a blizzard," Bobby said. "I never had enough snow to play in yet. Did you, Tess?"

"No, I never did," said Tess. "I wish we lived at the North Pole!"

Honey Bunch laughed, and that night, when she was cozily tucked in bed, she laughed some more. For she heard Tess and Bobby complaining because Teresa came into their rooms and raised the windows and shut off the steam heat.

"I freeze to pieces every morning!" grumbled Tess. "Leave the window down."

"Plenty of fresh air is good for you!" said

Teresa. "I thought you wanted to live at the North Pole!"

Honey Bunch snuggled down under the covers. Mother had put up the window in her room and had gone away to visit with Aunt Julia and Uncle Paul. Honey Bunch could feel the sweet, cold winter air coming in and she liked it.

"Aren't Tess and Bobby funny!" she giggled. "But they're nice."

CHAPTER VIII

A LITTLE LOST GIRL

ALAS, in the morning the snow was quite gone! Honey Bunch heard the sad news before she was out of bed, for Bobby was pattering about the hall in his bedroom slippers, wailing:

"I told you so! I knew it would be this way! There isn't one bit of snow left to play in!"

However, Bobby didn't feel bad very long and when he found there were hot cakes and maple syrup for breakfast he quite forgot the snow. He and Tess went happily off to school and they were hardly out of the door when Mrs. Morton said:

"Well, Honey Bunch, you and I are going shopping this morning."

Aunt Julia was putting on her hat even then, so Honey Bunch put on hers and stood

up on a chair and put the little hairpin in
Mother's veil just where she liked it to go.
Honey Bunch often helped Mother get ready
to go out.

"We're going shopping, Dorry," said
Honey Bunch, as they stepped into the elevator.

Dorry thought Honey Bunch was the nicest
little girl who had ever come to the apartment house. He told Tess so and she felt
very proud of her little cousin. Of course
Honey Bunch didn't know what Dorry
thought, but she liked him and she always
had something to tell him whenever she rode
in his elevator.

"You-all going to see the toys?" asked
Dorry now.

"Are we, Mother?" said Honey Bunch,
and when Mrs. Morton smiled and said she
thought they would look at the toys first,
Dorry smiled as merrily as Honey Bunch herself.

"Then you-all will have a good time," he
said kindly.

They walked to the corner again to wait for a bus, and this time when Honey Bunch saw one coming, she held up her hand and the great, wide bus drove in to the curb and stopped for them. There was one man riding on top, but he looked so cold and his nose was so red that Honey Bunch felt sorry for him. She was glad that her mother and aunt didn't want to ride outside.

Aunt Julia gave her the money and let her put it in the funny little box the conductor held out, and later she told her when to press the button that would stop the bus. Honey Bunch thought that Aunt Julia seemed to know exactly what a little girl would like to do.

"I s'pose it is because Tess is a little girl," Honey Bunch thought, poking her small thumb right into the middle of that black button.

They got out of the bus and had to cross the street to reach the large shop where Aunt Julia was taking them. The stream of automobiles went whizzing past and Honey Bunch hung back even when the whistle sounded and the traffic policeman held up his hand to keep the automobiles back.

"Come, dear," said Mrs. Morton. "The policeman says it is all right for us to cross. Nothing will hit us now."

But Honey Bunch stood still on the curb.

"Wait a minute," she begged. "Don't go yet, Mother."

Then that tall, straight policeman looked over and saw Honey Bunch trying to pull her mother and aunt back. All the automobiles, drawn up in a long line said "ha-ha-ha!" and Honey Bunch was sure that they would make a jump forward in just a minute. The traffic policeman didn't care how much the cars said ha-ha-ha! He walked across the street and came close to the curb.

"All right now," he said. "Come ahead."

Well, of course, it was all right then. Honey Bunch and her mother and her aunt walked straight over that crossing, in front of all those impatient automobiles and even a trolley car, and reached the other side without a bit of trouble. And the moment they were on the other curb, Toot! went the policeman's whistle, and every car jumped ahead.

It was a very large store into which Aunt Julia took them, and, goodness, every one else went, too. It was like the railroad terminal, Honey Bunch told Mother that night.

"Let's take the escalator," said Aunt Julia.

Honey Bunch thought she was talking about some kind of animal, but no, the escalator was moving stairs!

"Oh, Mother!" cried Honey Bunch, when she saw the stairs going up and up and people riding along on them without taking a step. "Oh, Mother, how can you slide down the banisters?"

"You don't," said Mrs. Morton, smiling. "Now, dear, be careful—don't try to walk; just keep your feet still."

Honey Bunch put out one foot, something bumped under her shoes and there she was, standing on a step and moving smoothly along like any one else.

"Isn't it nice?" she said, and the lady ahead of her heard and turned and smiled.

At the top of the stairs a pretty girl put out her hand and pulled Honey Bunch off. That was lucky, because the floor felt queer.

"I didn't know the floor was coming," said Honey Bunch, when to her surprise she found that she was off the stairway and standing on her own two feet on a red velvet carpet she had never seen before.

The toy department was on the fourth floor, and Honey Bunch had three lovely rides on the moving stairway before they came to the rows of dolls and the counters and counters of trains and games and tin wagons and other toys.

"What do you want to see first, Honey Bunch?" asked Aunt Julia.

"Dolls," said Honey Bunch. "All the dolls, Auntie, please."

There were big dolls and little dolls and dolls with party dresses and dolls all ready for kindergarten in dresses of gingham. Honey Bunch thought they were all beautiful.

"This is Anna Marie," said the clerk, taking a doll out of the show case and coming out from behind the counter to show her to Honey Bunch.

Anna Marie was almost as tall as Honey Bunch. The doll had long golden curls down to her waist, real eyelashes and a white pique frock with a patent leather belt exactly like the one that Honey Bunch wore.

"Ma-ma!" said Anna Marie. "Ma-ma!"

"Oh, Mother!" cried Honey Bunch. "Listen! What would Eleanor say?"

Eleanor, you know, was Honey Bunch's doll at home.

"She would like to take a little walk, I think," said the clerk, smiling. "You take her hand and I'll take the other and we'll give her a little walk around the floor."

Mrs. Morton slipped off Honey Bunch's coat, for the store was warm, and Honey Bunch took the doll's hand. And Anna Marie walked! She did indeed. She lifted up one foot in its patent leather slipper and pink silk sock and put it down and lifted up the other foot. And every time she lifted her foot, she took a step, just as Honey Bunch did.

"Look, Mother, look!" cried Honey Bunch. "She can walk!"

"Anna Marie can dance, too," said the clerk proudly. "Here, I'll play for you, and you dance a little with her."

The clerk sat down at a little toy piano and began a tinkly tune. Honey Bunch danced round and round with the big doll and Anna Marie kicked out her little feet and seemed to enjoy the fun. When the dance music stopped she stopped, too, and so did Honey Bunch.

"She is alive!" said the little girl, as she shook hands with Anna Marie and the clerk put her back in the glass case. "She must be alive, Mother! She can walk and talk the same as I do! Wouldn't it be fun to have a real, live doll to play with?"

They saw all the other toys before they went downstairs. Honey Bunch liked the doll houses and the dolls' furniture next to Anna Marie. But when her mother and aunt said they had shopping to do and took the elevator downstairs and began to look at net to make curtains for windows, Honey Bunch was very good and patient. She wasn't interested in net, but she sat quietly in a chair and waited for her mother and aunt to look at the curtains.

"I must get those pillow cases this morning," said Aunt Julia, when the net had been bought. "The linen department is on the next floor."

Down again they went and into the linen department where great stacks of sheets and pillow cases and tablecloths and napkins rose from the tables almost up to the ceiling.

There were no chairs to sit in here, so Honey Bunch walked around the tables as she waited for her mother and aunt to buy the pillow cases.

She found she could walk under some of the tables, and that was fun.

"I'm in a cave, a big lion's cave," said Honey Bunch, walking under one of the tables. "If a little girl comes along I'll growl at her."

But no little girl came past, and after Honey Bunch had crawled under several tables and walked around others, she thought she would go back and see if Aunt Julia was not through buying pillow cases.

Out from under the last table came Honey Bunch, but no mother and Aunt Julia were there. She was not in the linen department now, but another place, a place she had not seen before. There were beautiful soft, fur scarfs and muffs on the low tables and fur coats on the waxed figures standing around.

"Where's Mother?" said Honey Bunch softly. "I want my mother."

She went back to the tables and walked around them again, but she could not see her mother anywhere, or Aunt Julia, either. And no matter how many times she walked around the tables, she always came out at the same place, where the fur coats and scarfs were.

"Maybe Mother's lost," said Honey Bunch at last.

She sat down on the little platform where a wax lady stood and because she was only five years old and a pretty little girl to be all alone in a big department store in a big city, the tears began to trickle down her pink cheeks and splash into her lap.

"For goodness' sake, child, what's the matter?" asked an old lady, stopping suddenly. "Are you lost?"

"I can't—I can't find my mother!" sobbed Honey Bunch.

"Well, don't cry another drop," said the old lady kindly. "We'll see that you find your mother. You just come along with me."

Honey Bunch stood up and put her hand into the soft, wrinkled one the old lady held out to her. Straight up to a tall, dark-haired man the old lady walked and Honey Bunch with her.

"This child is lost," said the old lady. "Her mother's somewhere in the store. Will you look after her? I have to meet my daughter or I'd take care of her myself."

"We'll find your mother, little girl," said

the floorwalker. "We'll go up to the next floor and wait there; she'll come after you before very long."

Honey Bunch did not say anything. She trotted along beside the tall man and followed him into the elevator and out again, trying to keep up with the long steps he took. He led her into a quiet room with a great many green velvet chairs and sofas and ladies sitting and reading in some of them. There were little desks there, too, and some of the ladies were seated at these writing letters.

There was another old lady in this room, sitting at a table. She had curly white hair and did not wear a hat.

"She must live here," said Honey Bunch to herself.

"This little lady," said the floorwalker to the old lady, "can't find her mother. Will you look after her for a bit, Mrs. Bates?"

"Certainly I will," said Mrs. Bates, and she lifted Honey Bunch into a big chair near her.

The floorwalker went away and Honey

Bunch tried to smile at Mrs. Bates who opened her table drawer and took out three red gumdrops and gave them to her.

"Now all you have to do," said Mrs. Bates comfortably, "is to sit here and rest and by and by your mother will come."

"How will she know I am here?" asked Honey Bunch.

"All the lost children are brought here, and the first person your mother asks will tell her that," explained Mrs. Bates.

CHAPTER IX

VISITING THE FISH

HONEY BUNCH sat in the big green velvet chair and thought very hard. She wondered if other little lost girls had sat in that chair and if they felt as bad as she did. She wondered what would happen to her if her mother never came. How could she ever get home to Barham all by herself?

Then Honey Bunch wondered what happened to little girls whose mothers didn't come for them and who didn't know where they lived. There must be little girls, she thought, who couldn't even say "Barham" if asked where they lived. Honey Bunch knew a little girl who didn't talk plainly, though she was four years old.

"Maybe the policemen know where everybody lives," said Honey Bunch, at last.

She remembered the traffic officer who had

made the automobiles stand still while she crossed the street with Mother and Aunt Julia. Honey Bunch decided to ask him what to do if Mother didn't come and find her before Mrs. Bates had to go home and maybe leave her sitting there in the green velvet chair all night.

But Mother did come! She saw Honey Bunch first and ran—she didn't care how many people saw her—to the little girl sitting in the big chair.

"Oh, Mother!" cried Honey Bunch. "Mother! Where were you? I looked and I looked and I looked! I thought you were lost!"

"Lost, dearest!" said Mrs. Morton, hugging Honey Bunch at each word. "Why, you were lost, darling. My own little girl all alone in this great store! No wonder Mother was nearly frantic."

"We missed you in the linen department," Aunt Julia said, smiling at Honey Bunch. "We looked everywhere and we asked each clerk and no one had seen you. Your mother was afraid you had gone off to try the moving stairs again."

"Now, you see?" asked Mrs. Bates, smiling happily. "I told you if you waited here your mother would come. All lost little girls get found after a bit."

Honey Bunch was very glad to hear this and she shook hands with Mrs. Bates and said good-bye politely.

"But I would rather not be lost again," she said, as she and Mother and Aunt Julia were walking toward the elevator. "Even if you do get found."

"Lost again!" said Mrs. Morton. "You must never be lost again, sweetheart. Keep hold of Mother's hand and never, never try to go anywhere alone while we are in New York."

Well, you may be sure that Honey Bunch had plenty to tell Bobby and Tess and Uncle Paul that night. She had had lunch in the restaurant in the store with her mother and aunt, and they had gone to a concert afterward where Honey Bunch had had two little short naps when no one was looking. She did not see Bobby and Tess till nearly dinner time. They thought it would be fun to be lost, Bobby, especially.

"Nothing like that ever happens to me," he said almost sadly.

"I'm glad it doesn't," replied his mother, putting mashed potato on his plate. "It isn't fun to be lost, is it, Honey Bunch? And certainly no mother wants her little boy or girl lost."

"Do you think you will be too tired to go out to-morrow?" asked Mr. Turner. "Will Honey Bunch want to stay in bed and rest?"

Honey Bunch smiled. What a funny thing to say! She never wanted to stay in bed!

"I like to go out, Uncle Paul," she said. "Don't I, Mother?"

"I think you do," answered her mother, smiling.

"I thought perhaps you might like to come to see me, to-morrow," said Uncle Paul. "I can show you how New York looks when you are twenty-one stories above the automobiles and trolley cars."

"Oh, yes," cried Tess. "It's ever so much fun to go to Daddy's office. Come on, Bobby, we can skip geography to-morrow."

Every one laughed. Tess was so ready to "skip" geography and a day in school. Honey Bunch wished she were old enough to go to school, but Tess would rather play. She said so.

"You and Bobby are going with Honey Bunch to the matinee Saturday and that will have to make up to you for to-morrow," said Mr. Turner firmly. "I don't know what your mother plans for the morning, but I should like to take my niece to lunch about half-past one."

"We'll meet you at your office at one o'clock," planned Aunt Julia. "I want to take Honey Bunch down to the Aquarium in the morning and then we'll come right up."

"Oh, Mother! You said you wouldn't take Honey Bunch on the subway till we could go," cried Bobby. "We want to see her ride

first, Mother. She was so sure the subways
were a man! Don't you remember, Mother?"

Mrs. Turner laughed. She remembered
what Tess and Bobby had told her when they
came home from Honey Bunch's birthday
party. Mr. Subways was the name of a man
who came to see the daddy of Honey Bunch
and no amount of talking could make the
little girl understand that "subways" were
underground railroads.

"All right, to please you, Bobby," said Mrs.
Turner, "I'll go to Daddy's office on the ele-
vated. The surface cars are out of the question, they're so slow. You and Tess shall go
along when we first take Honey Bunch in the
subway."

Honey Bunch was so excited at all this
talk that she was sure she needn't go to bed.
She could sit up and play soldiers with Bobby
and Tess till breakfast time, she knew she
could. But her mother said no, she must go
to bed like a good girl, and, dear me, she was
asleep the moment she put her yellow head
on her pillow.

"Tess and I have to work all the time," sighed Bobby, the next morning.

"When you were five years old you were doing just what Honey Bunch is doing now," said his mother, kissing him. "I took you and Tess and we went visiting and you didn't go to school but played all day long. When Honey Bunch is as old as you are, she will go to school every day and study hard, too. Won't you, dear?"

"Yes, I will," replied Honey Bunch, nodding her head vigorously. "I'm going to learn to play the piano like Tess and have a 'rithmetic book like Bobby's."

The twins went off to school as soon as breakfast was over, and Uncle Paul went to his office, first telling Honey Bunch not to forget she was to come to see him.

"Don't let your mother or Aunt Julia get so interested in pink leather shoes they forget to bring you," he said solemnly.

"We're going to the Aquarium, not shopping," Aunt Julia said. "Honey Bunch must see the queer fish."

It was a beautiful day, clear and cold and
sunny. Aunt Julia said, as soon as she sniffed
that nice fresh air when she and Honey
Bunch and Mrs. Morton left the apartment
house, that she thought they would all enjoy
the ride down to the Battery on the surface
cars.

"Oh, yes, let's ride on the surface cars," said
Honey Bunch. "I never rode on any."

But after all, the surface cars were trolley
cars! They were not exactly like trolley cars
Honey Bunch had seen and they opened in
the middle—which was fun because it was just
like walking into a room—and when you sat
down you could look into the wagons and
automobiles that were passing.

"Only they're trolley cars," said Honey
Bunch, to herself. "I'll tell Ida Camp they
say 'surface cars' when they mean trolley cars
in New York."

They had to change cars twice, but at last
they came to the Battery. Honey Bunch was
delighted to see the water, though such a cold

wind came blowing across it that Aunt Julia
hurried them into the Aquarium as fast as
she could.

"Is this the house where the fish live?"
asked Honey Bunch.

Mother had told her a little about the fish
and that the building where she was to see
them had once been an old fort, and then a
concert hall. Honey Bunch had been quite
sure that she would see the fish housekeeping.
She thought perhaps a fish in a white apron
and cap, like Teresa's, would open the door
for them.

She thought she knew exactly how a fish
would look running a carpet sweeper and she
would not have been in the least surprised
to see a Daddy fish walking out of the door
with his hat and coat on to go to his office,
or a Doctor fish coming in with his black
bag to give the fish children pills to make
them well again.

But Honey Bunch forgot to be disappointed when she saw the curious fish swim-

ming lazily around in their tanks. Some of them were beautiful colors—like a rainbow— and some were as flat as pancakes and others so fat they looked as though they might burst.

"He's solid gold, isn't he, Mother?" said Honey Bunch, pointing to one lovely gold fish that had a tank all to himself.

It wasn't solid gold, but it was the color of solid gold and Honey Bunch liked to look at the pretty thing.

The tanks in which these fish lived were of glass and set into the wall so that people could look at them as they would at pictures hanging on the wall. Upstairs, besides the tanks of fish, there were glass cases of lovely corals and anemones and crabs and odd growing things. Honey Bunch had to be lifted up to look at these things and she said she liked the fish better.

"Now I am sure we have seen every single fish there is," announced Aunt Julia at last, "and if we are going to get uptown and meet Paul, we should start now."

The ride uptown—well, that was exciting.

First they climbed so many iron stairs that Honey Bunch was sure even Bobby couldn't count them, and Bobby said he could count as high as any boy in his school. Then they went through a little clicking gate and came out on a platform away above the street.

"This must be as high up as Uncle Paul's office," said Honey Bunch, looking down at the people walking on the pavement.

"Oh, this isn't far up," answered Aunt Julia. "Come, dear, here is our train. We must hurry."

In the train Honey Bunch stared out of the window every minute of the ride. No wonder—she was seeing into people's houses! She saw a little girl having her hair brushed in one house and a little boy eating out of a bowl in another house and a woman leaning so far out of a window a little further along that Honey Bunch was sure she would tumble out in a minute—but Aunt Julia said no, she would be careful.

Honey Bunch saw pink and green and blue dresses hung up to dry; she saw men painting a large sign, on the roof of a house; she saw people sewing and hammering and making things—she looked at it all through their front windows high above the street.

"I like the high-up railroad," she told Mother, as they got out at the right station and followed Aunt Julia down the steep iron stairs.

CHAPTER X

"Now hold fast to my hand," said Mother, as they came to a busy street.

Honey Bunch was quite sure they would never get across that street. An express wagon went rattling past, the two large gray horses running, the driver flourishing his whip and a little black dog, high up on the seat beside him, barking so hard that Honey Bunch was afraid he would bark himself right off the seat.

But when two automobiles turned, she saw a tall policeman standing in the middle of the street.

"He'll make them stop," she said comfortably.

Sure enough, in a few minutes his whistle sounded and the automobiles and wagons stopped. Mother and Aunt Julia and Honey

Bunch walked across the street and found themselves at the door of the building where Aunt Julia said Uncle Paul had his office.

"And nothing ran over us," said Honey Bunch, with a little sigh of relief.

She liked this big city of New York, oh, very much. But she told Mother as they went into the elevator in Uncle Paul's building that she liked to cross the streets in Barham better.

"I feel bigger at home," she explained. "And there's more room for me."

Aunt Julia laughed and said there wasn't much room for any one in New York. But she must have meant in the streets, for the big elevator in which they were slowly going up was large enough for twenty little girls like Honey Bunch.

Up, up, they went slowly; and Honey Bunch thought the elevator seemed tired because it had so far to go. She whispered this to Mother, but the elevator man heard her and smiled.

"If I shot you up to the twenty-first floor,

Miss," he said, "you'd be sick and dizzy and out of breath. It's safer and better to go sailing through the air than to go shooting—you take my word for it."

"I will," Honey Bunch promised him gravely. "I don't like shooting anyway. I always close my eyes."

They had reached the twenty-first floor now and the elevator man stopped the car and opened the iron grating for them.

"We go down to the end of the corridor," said Aunt Julia leading them down to a glass door with a great many black letters on it.

When she opened the door for a minute Honey Bunch blinked her eyes. She was looking directly into the strong sunshine which came through four great windows. There were several young women in the room and their typewriters were making a clicking noise.

"Good morning," said Aunt Julia to the pretty girl who came forward to speak to her. "I believe Mr. Turner expects us."

The typewriters went on clicking, but Honey Bunch found that every one was looking at her. She smiled and pressed closer to the railing, which was like a little fence with a gate in the middle. The pretty girl had come through this gate to see Aunt Julia.

"What's your name, dear?" asked the young woman whose desk was nearest to her.

"Honey Bunch," said Honey Bunch politely.

"Well, I have something good for you," said the young woman opening her top drawer and taking out two caramels. "Do you like candy?"

"Thank you," said Honey Bunch, making her little curtsey. "But I have to ask Mother 'fore I eat things."

She turned around and Mother and Aunt Julia were not there!

"They went down into Mr. Turner's offices," said the young woman who had offered Honey Bunch the caramels. "Here comes Miss Hunter after you."

"Your mother is waiting for you," said Miss Hunter, coming up to Honey Bunch. "I'll show you where she is."

Honey Bunch called "Good-bye," and the girls at the typewriters waved to her. Then she trotted after Miss Hunter down a little hall and into a handsome office where her mother and Aunt Julia were sitting in two large leather-covered chairs.

"We'll have to wait a few minutes for Uncle," said Aunt Julia.

Miss Hunter went away and Honey Bunch kneeled on a chair and looked at the pictures in a magazine which was on the long table. She found a picture of a little girl who looked like Tess, she thought, and as she was looking at it suddenly two hands were put tightly over her eyes.

"Guess who it is," said a kind, laughing voice.

"Uncle Paul!" cried Honey Bunch.

It was Uncle Paul and he lifted her down from the chair and said he was very glad to see her.

"I think we're all very hungry," said Aunt Julia, smiling.

"I want to show Edith and Honey Bunch the view from my window and then we'll go out to lunch at once," answered Uncle Paul. "Come, chicken, tell me what you think of New York from here."

They all followed Uncle Paul into a large square room and over to the window that filled almost one side of it. Honey Bunch looked down and away, away, far below her, she saw little black things scurrying about.

"People!" cried Honey Bunch. "Are they people, Uncle Paul?"

"Yes, dear," he said. "People and horses and automobiles down in the streets. You couldn't hear a man shout from here, and he couldn't hear you if you called to him."

"Mother, look 'way down," urged Honey Bunch.

"I am looking, dear," said her mother. "Think of the men who could build a tall building like this!"

Honey Bunch stood quietly at the window

a little while, looking at the street so far below her and at the red and green and rusty looking roofs of buildings which were not as tall as the one she was in. Pigeons were flying about these roofs and Uncle Paul told her that many of the birds lived in houses on the roofs.

"I should think they'd rather live in the country," said Honey Bunch. "I don't think a pigeon has much fun on the roof. There isn't any garden for him to play in."

"Well, if we are going to lunch, let's go," said Uncle Paul, putting a heavy block of glass on the papers he had been looking at while Honey Bunch looked out of the window. "Honey Bunch, where would you like to go? You are my honor guest to-day."

This sounded very nice and it was even nicer to see Uncle Paul say it. His eyes crinkled up and he patted the little hand Honey Bunch slipped into his as though he was very proud to have an honor guest in his office.

He didn't give Honey Bunch time to answer, though, because he took a key out of his pocket and opened a door that led out into the hall opposite another elevator, not the one they had come up in, and another elevator man stopped to take them on.

"Oh, oh!" said Honey Bunch, as the car started. "I guess he must be shooting. I would rather sail!"

She felt so queer that she hid her face in Mother's coat, but it wasn't long before they were on the ground floor and Honey Bunch found the queer feeling had gone. Mother told her that very often grown-up people felt a little queer when they went down in an elevator.

Honey Bunch walked with Uncle Paul, and Mother and Aunt Julia walked together. They had not far to go till they came to a restaurant and Uncle Paul held open the door and they all went in. A waiter came up to them, a nice waiter with white hair, and he was so smiling and he bowed so politely that Honey Bunch made him a little curtsey.

There were a good many people seated at the tables, eating, and they laughed, but it did

not sound as though they were laughing at
Honey Bunch. She smiled back at them and
some one threw her a lovely soft pink rose.
Uncle Paul picked it up for her and she trotted after him and the waiter over to a beautiful round table set in the window where
she could see the people walking in the
street.

"I'll attend to this young lady," said the
white-haired waiter when two others came
hurrying up.

And he did. He told the other waiters
what to do for Mother and Aunt Julia and
Uncle Paul, but he pulled out a chair for
Honey Bunch himself and he lifted her into
it and he helped her take off her coat and tie
a napkin over her dress so that nothing should
spot it.

The chair wasn't quite high enough, and
he found another chair for her. Then, when
she was all nicely settled, he went away and
later the tall thin waiter who had been bringing water and menu cards and helping Mother
and Aunt Julia with their coats, brought

them the good things to eat that Uncle Paul ordered.

Everywhere Honey Bunch looked, she saw smiling faces. Presently soft music began somewhere. Honey Bunch looked and looked and by and by she saw the piano back of green palms and a man with a violin playing. It was very lovely.

"What would you rather have for dessert, Honey Bunch?" asked Uncle Paul when dessert time came.

"Ice-cream, please," said Honey Bunch promptly.

"What kind?" he asked her seriously.

There was a silver vase on the table filled with pink roses. Honey Bunch knew what kind of ice-cream she wanted when she looked at them.

"Pink, please," she said.

They had pink ice-cream and little cakes with pink icing and when that was all gone it was time to go. The white-haired waiter came up to their table when he saw them getting ready to leave. He took the pretty pink roses out of their silver vase, dried the stems on a napkin and handed them to Honey Bunch.

"You're very kind to us," said Uncle Paul, smiling.

"The little lady can have anything in this place," said the waiter, looking at Honey Bunch, who was hugging her pink roses close to her brown coat.

"Thank you for the flowers," said Honey Bunch clearly. "And if you ever come to Barham you can have some of the roses in our garden—can't he, Mother?"

Mrs. Morton said yes indeed, and then they walked down the strip of green carpet that led them straight to the front door.

"I must go back, for there's a conference at three," said Uncle Paul to Aunt Julia. "Are you going straight home?"

"Straight home," answered Aunt Julia. "And we'll walk over and take the bus. I don't dare take Honey Bunch on the subway till the children are with us. They made me promise."

So Honey Bunch had another ride on the
bus, which she liked very much, and when
they reached the apartment house Aunt Julia
remembered that she wanted to get a head
of lettuce for dinner.

"You run in, Honey Bunch, because I am
sure Tess and Bobby are at home," said Aunt
Julia, "and your mother and I will walk over
to the avenue grocery store. We won't be
gone long and you children can play till we
come back."

Honey Bunch ran into the hall, ready to
ask Dorry to take her up. But some one else
was ringing the elevator bell. Some one she
remembered, though she didn't know his
name.

CHAPTER XI

LESTER MORRIS

HONEY BUNCH stopped running when she saw this some one. She backed away. She would have run back to her mother, only she didn't exactly want to run away. The some one ringing the elevator bell was the boy on the train who had made faces at her!

He made a face the minute he saw Honey Bunch now, a dreadful face. He stuck out his tongue and rolled his eyes and looked as bad as he possibly could.

"Hello!" he said. "What are you doing here, missy?"

"I'm—I'm visiting my cousins," replied Honey Bunch.

"I'm sorry for 'em, then," said this bad boy, giving the bell another deep push.

"Dorry doesn't like you to ring the bell too much," Honey Bunch said gravely. "He

can't hurry when he's at the top of the house.
He said so."

"He'd better hurry, if he knows what's
good for him," declared the bad boy, making
another face at Honey Bunch. "My father
will have him discharged if he doesn't hurry
when I ring this bell."

"Does your father own this house?" asked
Honey Bunch, wishing Dorry would hurry.
She didn't think the boy would make faces
at her if there was some one else there to
see how he behaved.

"My father wouldn't own this house," said
the boy, ringing the bell again. "We live
on the fifth floor, and if we don't get what
we want we move and then the owner has to
find some one else to rent his old apartment."

"Well, if you-all don't quit ringing that
bell, you-all will have to rent another apartment," cried the angry Dorry, flinging open
the iron gate and staring at the bad boy crossly.
"Guess you think you-all is the only person in
the whole house, don't you?"

"I'm in a hurry. I have to get my roller

skates," said the bad boy, trying to push past
Dorry and get into the elevator. "Get out
of the way, Dorry, I have to hurry—the boys
are waiting for me."

"I don't care nothing 'bout boys," said
Dorry, putting his arm across the door so that
the boy could not get in. "I'm only taking
ladies this trip. Come on, Miss Honey Bunch,
you-all want to go up?"

He stood aside to let Honey Bunch in the
car then slipped in after her and closed the
gate with a bang so sharply that it almost
nipped the nose of the bad boy.

"I'll fix you!" cried the boy. "You'll be
sorry. I'll tell the superintendent we never
get any service in this place."

"You might just use the stairs if you want
those roller skates," said Dorry calmly, start-
ing the car.

The bad boy made a terrific face at them
through the iron grating before they lost
sight of him.

"Don't pay no attention to that Lester Morris," said Dorry to Honey Bunch. "He makes

a lot of noise, but he can't do anything. He's just disagreeable, that's all."

Honey Bunch got off at the fourth floor and Dorry, instead of going back for Lester, went on up. Honey Bunch found Tess and Bobby waiting for her, but although they had a fine game of train with the chairs for the cars, Honey Bunch couldn't stop thinking about the bad boy, Lester.

"I wish he didn't live here," she said to Mother that night, when she was being undressed for bed. "I don't see why he has to live here!"

"Why, my dear little girl," said Mrs. Morton, with a kiss, "don't let that bad boy worry you. You won't have to see him often, and he doesn't play with Bobby and Tess. I think he must be older than they are. You may not even hear of him again before we go home. Don't think of unpleasant things, darling; think of all the happy things you know have happened and are going to happen."

"All right, I will," said Honey Bunch, like

the sensible little girl she really was. "I'll
think about to-morrow."

Honey Bunch knew that she and Mother
and Aunt Julia were going shopping the next
day again and that the day after that would
be Saturday and she and Bobby and Tess
were going to a matinee. Surely that was
enough for any little girl to think about, and
Honey Bunch was thinking as fast as she
could when she fell asleep and never thought
about anything at all till the next morning.

"We're going to a store for little girls and
boys this morning," said Aunt Julia, when
she and Mother and Honey Bunch were in
the bus.

Honey Bunch could wave to the busses now
and make them stop. She wasn't quite so
afraid to cross a street as she had been at first.
She liked to ride in elevators.

"We'll make a New Yorker of you yet,"
said Uncle Paul, when he wanted to tease her.

The store for little boys and girls was a
wonderful and lovely place. There was
everything there that a little boy or girl could

ever wear and things for the tiny, tiny baby
to wear, too. There were a great many fat
little boys and girls there with their mothers,
trying on coats and dresses and shoes. Honey
Bunch liked to watch them, especially one little boy who wouldn't go away from the long
mirror. He liked to stand and stare at himself so much that he wouldn't move when his
mother wanted him to try on another coat.
The clerk had to take it off and put another
one on while the little boy stood and stared
into the glass.

Honey Bunch watched him till his mother
said he must go home with her. Then that
little boy cried and hung on to the mirror
and had to be dragged away. Every one
laughed and said what a vain little boy he
must be.

Upstairs there were charming dresses for
little girls and Honey Bunch tried on some
while Mother and Aunt Julia watched her.
The very prettiest of all was a blue linen,
just the color of Honey Bunch's blue eyes.
It was made with a little round white yoke

which was hemstitched to the dress and the hem was hemstitched, too. Just above the hem were embroidered white daisies.

"Do you like that dress, dearie?" asked Aunt Julia, putting her arm around Honey Bunch.

"It's the nicest dress!" said Honey Bunch. "It has a black velvet tie in back."

"So it has," agreed Aunt Julia. "I think it is a pretty dress, too—much too pretty to go away and leave. I think I'll have to buy it for a dear little girl I know—a little girl I love very much."

Honey Bunch looked a little puzzled.

"It's a present from Auntie, dear," explained Aunt Julia. "With my love."

Then Honey Bunch knew that Aunt Julia was buying the dress for her and she kissed her and thanked her and told her how much she loved her. The clerk took off the pretty dress and they had it sent to the apartment, because Aunt Julia said they wouldn't want to carry even a pretty dress around with them.

"Now I'm as sorry as I can be, but I must go to a meeting," said Aunt Julia, when the dress had been put in a box and the clerk was told where to send it. "I'd much rather be with you two, but it can't be helped."

"Honey Bunch and I are going to take a walk," said Mrs. Morton. "We haven't had a real walk in a week. It isn't cold to-day and we'll enjoy a little fresh air."

So at the corner Aunt Julia left them and Honey Bunch and Mother went down one of the long, narrow streets for their walk.

They saw ever so many things to interest them in the windows. There was one window filled with little queer carvings from China, and another with ribbons and silks, the gayest colors Honey Bunch had ever seen.

"Oh, Mother, look across the street!" she cried, pointing to a window. "Birds, Mother! And they're alive!"

The birds were as bright-colored as the ribbons and twice as interesting. There were red birds and green birds and black and white ones. Some hopped cheerfully about, some

sat on their perches and looked solemn, and
some stood huddled in a corner of their cages
and never moved a feather.

"I wish I could let them out, Mother," said
kind little Honey Bunch. "I don't believe
they have one bit good time. They would
rather be out on the trees, even if it is winter.
I think it must be hot to be in a little cage
on top of another cage."

"Well, dear, I wouldn't put any bird in a
cage, either," replied Mrs. Morton. "But
these little birds are used to it now and they
couldn't live out in the streets. Cats would
catch them. I think they are happier in the
window, sweetheart."

But Honey Bunch still felt sorry for the
birds. She thought they were homesick for
the trees and the outdoors, even the winter
outdoors. The cages were small, and if a
bird didn't want people to stare at it, it
couldn't help it. Honey Bunch thought
there ought to be a lace curtain or something,
for bird houses. They had curtains at home
in Barham. Her mother said she did not

like strangers to look into the house through the front windows.

"Look in this window, dear," said Mrs. Morton.

That other window made Honey Bunch forget the birds, for it was filled with fat, happy puppies who rolled about and played and bit each other and had a beautiful time. One came up to the window and looked at Honey Bunch through the glass. When she tapped her finger, the puppy tried to bite it and fell over backward.

"Oh, Mother, what dear little dogs!" cried Honey Bunch. "Look at that one in the corner—and that brown one asleep in the basket—and the spotted one biting his brother. Is that his brother, Mother?"

Mrs. Morton said she thought it was the puppy's brother and she and Honey Bunch stood and watched the puppies till it was time to think of lunch. They had a nice lunch together and they went home, and while her mother wrote to her daddy, Honey Bunch played outdoors with Tess and Bobby and

Kenneth Evans, who were home from school by that time.

"Give my love to Daddy and tell him to take some to Lady Clare," said Honey Bunch before she went out to play. "And tell him we saw the puppies in the window."

"Hurrah, it's Saturday!" shouted Bobby the next morning at the breakfast table. He was so excited that he upset the cream jug and Uncle Paul said if it hadn't been Saturday he would have had to leave the table.

"I suppose this is a great day and we have to make excuses," Uncle Paul said, while Bobby looked sorry. "What are you children going to do?"

"Going to see 'Gold Heart,' Daddy," said Bobby. "It's at the Lyon Theater and Honey Bunch has never been to the theater. And we're coming home on the subway."

"Well, I hope the two mothers can stand the fun," said Uncle Paul, patting Honey Bunch on the head. She sat next to him. "I should say that taking three children to see a play was an undertaking."

"Lester Morris is going, too," declared Bobby. "He told me so last night. I met him in the elevator."

Honey Bunch was sorry to hear this, but she didn't think about Lester long. She thought about the theater instead. That was pleasanter.

CHAPTER XII

THE FAIRY PLAY

TESS and Bobby thought the afternoon was never going to come. To make the time before lunch go faster—for their mother said she didn't want them to go out and play or Honey Bunch might get tired—the twins told Honey Bunch about the theater.

"It's all light when you go in," said Bobby. "And you sit down and the music plays. Then, all of a sudden, the lights go out and it's pitch dark."

"Then the great, big curtain rolls up," said Tess, "and——"

"Who rolls it up?" interrupted Honey Bunch excitedly.

"Oh, some one," said Tess. "Men back of the stage, I guess. Anyway, it goes up and you see the stage and people walk on it and talk and that's the play. Some of the girls go to the theater every week, but Mother won't let us. We haven't been once since last winter."

Tess's mother heard her and smiled.

"If you went every week, Tess dear," she said, "you'd soon find out that you can get tired of the theater, like everything else. When you are grown up and have a little girl of your own I don't believe you will want her to go to a matinee every Saturday."

Well, they had lunch at last and then Honey Bunch put on her new blue linen dress Aunt Julia had given her and her pretty coat and hat and Tess put on her velvet dress and her best coat and hat, too, and Bobby brushed his hair again. He already had on his best suit, and he looked very nice indeed.

"Now we're going," said Honey Bunch, as her mother and Aunt Julia came out into the hall where the three children were prancing around the elevator door.

Mrs. Morton laughed and pressed the button.

"I don't know whether I should let you go

without being tied to me, Honey Bunch," she said. "You're so excited you might float up into the air, and then how should I get you down?"

Dorry, who had brought the elevator up, grinned cheerfully.

"Shall I get a piece of string, Miz Morton?" he asked. "You could tie Miss Honey Bunch to your coat button."

Honey Bunch looked down at her small shoes. Then she stood on tiptoe.

"I won't float, Mother," she said earnestly. "I can hold on by my toes."

But Bobby and Tess, when they were out on the street, put Honey Bunch between them and Bobby held one hand and Tess the other. They didn't believe their little cousin was going to float away like a kite, but they thought it would be safer to help hold her down.

They took the surface car—that opened in the middle, as Honey Bunch said—to reach the theater, and, though she looked around carefully, Honey Bunch could not see Lester

Morris. She had been afraid he would sit near them and perhaps make faces at her all through the play.

"See the lights?" whispered Tess, as soon as they were inside and their coats were off and they were seated in a row.

Honey Bunch sat next to her mother and Aunt Julia sat next to Mrs. Morton with Bobby on one side of her. Tess was on the other side of Honey Bunch.

The theater was blazing with bright lights and people were rustling in, laughing and talking. Honey Bunch saw little boys and girls and their grandmas and mothers and aunties. Every one seemed to be having a beautiful time.

"Like the music?" whispered Bobby, leaning across his mother so that Honey Bunch could hear him.

Honey Bunch nodded. She liked it all, the lights and music and people, the noise and laughter. The big fire curtain on the stage rolled up, up, out of sight. Suddenly the lights went out. Honey Bunch felt for Mother's hand.

"It's all right, darling," whispered Mother. "Watch the curtain. See, it is going up!"

The beautiful red velvet curtain was being pulled back. And then every child in the house said "Ah!" for the handsome prince, "Gold Heart," was on the stage and his sword clinked as he walked over to the window and flung it wide open.

It was a fairy play and Tess had told Honey Bunch that 'most anything could happen in a fairy play. So Honey Bunch wasn't surprised to see an old fairy come hobbling in through the window; that is, she was an old, old woman because she didn't want every one to know that she was a fairy. She told Gold Heart that she had heard all about him and how he wanted to kill the wicked giant who frightened and hurt his people.

"Would you like me to help you?" asked the fairy.

Gold Heart thought she was an old woman

who couldn't help any one, but he was polite and said yes.

"Take this gold cap, then," said the old woman, "and wear it. Nothing can hurt you as long as you have it on."

So she gave the prince a cap of solid gold and he put it on and it fitted him perfectly. The old woman fairy went away and the prince sat down to read a book by the open window.

"Look!" whispered Tess, giving Honey Bunch such a poke that she nearly pushed her off her seat. "Look! Somebody's coming in at the window!"

Goodness! Honey Bunch was as excited as Tess. The prince had his back to the window, and there, climbing in over the yellow roses that grew around the sill, was the ugliest little dwarf you ever saw!

Bobby leaned across his mother's lap to whisper to Honey Bunch.

"I'll bet he wants to steal that gold cap," he said.

That was just what that dwarf wanted to

do! He crept in so carefully that the prince didn't hear him at all. Down to the floor he jumped and crept softly around the table. He put up his hand to take the cap and still the prince went on reading.

"He's got it!" shrieked Honey Bunch. "He's got the cap! Stop him, quick! I saw him steal it!"

The dwarf jumped up and leaped through the window with the precious cap, the curtain came down with a soft thud, and the lights shone again. All around Honey Bunch people were laughing, but she was so excited that she was still jumping up and down and begging some one to stop the dwarf.

"It's only a play, dear," said Mrs. Morton. "Don't bounce around like that. It's make-believe. You mustn't spoil the play by making such a noise."

"That prince will get his cap back all right—you'll see," said the wise Bobby.

And the prince did. Honey Bunch was dreadfully worried for fear the dwarf would run off and hide and the gold cap would never

be found. But in the very next act the prince
was out in the woods and he met an elf who
gave him a bag and told him what to say when
he met the dwarf. All the prince had to do
then was to say these magic words when he
found the dwarf, take his gold cap, and tie
the bad dwarf up in the bag and leave him
in the woods. And in the third and last act,
the prince wore his cap of gold and found
the giant who was making all his people un-
happy.

The prince and the giant met on a high
cliff and you could hear the ocean roaring
down below the cliff although you could not
see it. Of course the giant couldn't hurt the
prince when he wore his gold cap, and Gold
Heart took his sword and knocked that wicked
giant over backward, down, down into the
ocean.

"Hear him splash!" cried Honey Bunch in
great glee, as the giant landed in the water.

That was the end of the play and every one
got ready to go home. There were so many
people in the aisles that no one could walk

fast and Honey Bunch was so pushed and pulled that she stepped on some one's foot before she could help it. She turned around to say, "Excuse me," and there was Lester Morris, the boy who liked to make faces.

"Did you see the prince knock the giant down into the ocean?" asked Honey Bunch, who was still thinking about the play.

"Huh, that's nothing!" said Lester. "I could knock that giant down all by myself. I don't think he was much of a giant."

"Why, the idea!" sputtered Honey Bunch. "You couldn't, either! I don't believe any one could knock a giant down unless the fairies told him how to do it."

"You couldn't knock a fly down, Lester!" said Bobby. "I'd like to see you try to punch a giant. He would pick you up and throw you into his dungeon and you'd never get out."

"You show me a giant and I'll let you see whether I can knock him down or not," retorted Lester, but of course Bobby didn't

know where there was a giant. Neither did
Lester, for that matter.

Lester was with another boy and an older
cousin and they went off before Bobby and
Honey Bunch and Tess had their coats fastened. Bobby could hardly wait to show his
cousin the subway.

"Let me put the money in, Mother," he
begged, and Mrs. Turner gave him the
change and let him go down the long stairs
first.

"You go through," said Bobby to his
mother, when they were in the station.

Honey Bunch stared at the funny little
arms which made a rattling noise when people pushed past them. Bobby dropped nick-
els in the slot; clank, clank, went those queer
wooden arms; and they all stood on the other
side, on a cement platform.

Honey Bunch stared about her. There
were no windows anywhere, just electric
lights. Aunt Julia held Bobby back from the
edge of the platform, but he pointed out to

Honey Bunch different colored lights, red and blue and green, that winked.

"Here comes the train!" cried Tess, as they heard a rumbling noise.

A long string of cars rushed by them without any engine. At least Honey Bunch didn't see any engine, but Bobby told her that the engineer was in the first car and that he didn't need an engine because it was an electric train.

At first Honey Bunch thought the train was not going to stop to take them on. But it did before all the cars had gone past the spot where they stood on the platform.

Bobby wanted to go into the first car and look at the tracks through the glass door, but the train was so crowded his mother said she thought they had better stay where they were. A man gave Mrs. Morton his seat and Aunt Julia stood up with the children beside the sliding door to see that Bobby didn't let them get off at the wrong station, she said.

"It's dark," said Honey Bunch, as the train

left the station and she found she couldn't see anything.

"We're under the ground, dear," explained Aunt Julia. "Away down under the pavements and buildings, you know. All the subways are built underground. See how fast we are going!"

The train made so much noise that it was hard to talk, but Honey Bunch stood on her tiptoes and shouted a question.

"Is it named for Mr. Subways?" she cried. "He came to see us at Barham."

Aunt Julia smiled and shook her head. That meant no. Honey Bunch was puzzled, but then there were lots of queer things in New York. She stared out at the lighted stations they passed and watched the people get on and off at the stations where the train stopped. In a few minutes Bobby said it was their turn to get off and they all squeezed through the door, went through the funny little arms—only this time no one had to put any money in the slot—and up the stairs out into the street.

Honey Bunch stopped and looked back down the iron stairs.

"Well, dearie," said her mother, "what do you think of riding on the subway? Did you like it?"

Honey Bunch nodded.

"I *like* it, Mother," she said. "But I didn't see any potatoes."

Bobby stared at her. The others, too, for that matter.

CHAPTER XIII

MISS DOROTHY'S PARTY

"POTATOES?" Bobby cried. "Who said anything about potatoes? Aren't you silly, Honey Bunch!"

"I am not silly!" declared Honey Bunch. "I guess I know that potatoes and cabbages and things like that are in cellars, Bobby Turner! And Aunt Julia said we went right under the buildings—right through people's cellars. I was watching to see their potatoes and cabbages. We have potatoes in our cellar at home."

Bobby and Tess laughed, but Aunt Julia patted Honey Bunch's cheek.

"Don't mind these silly children, Honey Bunch," she said. "They laugh at everything. I daresay you would have seen potatoes and cabbages in the cellars if the subway

hadn't a little tunnel of its own to go through.
You see, dear, when they built the subway for
the cars to run in, they made a tunnel for the
tracks. No one can see outside the tunnel
walls. Ask Uncle Paul about it. He will explain better than I can."

But Honey Bunch forgot about the subway
and Bobby and Tess forgot to laugh at her
when they reached the apartment and found
that the postman had left three blue letters
for them. Honey Bunch was sure hers must
be from her daddy.

"No, it isn't," cried Tess, opening her letter and pulling out the little blue card in it
so hurriedly that she tore the corner. " 'Tisn't
from your daddy, Honey Bunch. It's dancing
school and we're going to have a party
Wednesday afternoon. Miss Dorothy said
so."

Honey Bunch couldn't read her card, but
her mother read it to her. Sure enough, Miss
Dorothy had invited her to the party Wednesday afternoon.

"How did she know I was here?" asked

Honey Bunch, much astonished. "She didn't see me come."

Uncle Paul, who had reached home ahead of them, pulled Honey Bunch into his lap.

"I suspect that Miss Dorothy knows all about you, Honey Bunch," he said. "Bobby and Tess have been talking about your visit ever since Christmas. I hope you will bring me home a cake; I never get asked to these parties. I like pink icing best, remember."

"Now, Paul," said Honey Bunch's mother, "don't tell Honey Bunch things like that. How can I teach her that it isn't polite to bring home cake from a party when you ask for it?"

But Uncle Paul only laughed and kissed Honey Bunch and tickled Tess till she doubled up on the sofa. Then he went off to read his paper till dinner was ready.

The children talked about the party from that Saturday night till Wednesday morning. Kenneth Evans was going and so, alas! was Lester Morris.

"He's as bad as he can be in dancing class!"

scolded Tess. "I don't see why he comes to the party. He doesn't like girls—he said so."

"Well, Tess, I wouldn't fret, if I were you," said Aunt Julia. "I'm sure Lester likes to go to a party as much as you do. Perhaps if you think more kindly of him, he'll behave better."

"No, Mother," said Bobby seriously, "he's only going because he heard Miss Dorothy say there would be two kinds of ice-cream. He doesn't like parties, only the ice-cream part."

Bobby himself was more interested in the ice-cream than in the party, though he didn't say so. He went to dancing school because his daddy said all boys should know how to dance. Bobby usually danced with Tess unless Miss Dorothy made him ask some other little girl. Then he said he didn't like dancing school.

This party was the most exciting one Honey Bunch had ever been invited to. She knew it was as soon as Tess told her that it was to

be in a hotel and that her mother was going
to take them in a taxicab.

"We can't go in the subway, because it is
too far to walk," said Tess. "Anyway, I'll
have on my new slippers."

"I have new slippers," said Honey Bunch.
"Mother bought them."

Honey Bunch's slippers were pink kid and
she had a pink dress and pink silk socks.
Dear me, how dressed up she did feel
Wednesday afternoon! Tess did, too. Tess
wore a white dress with blue slippers and
socks. She sat in a chair as soon as she was
dressed and wouldn't move.

"Something 'most always happens to me,"
said Tess. "But it won't this time."

She meant that she raced around so and was
so careless that she usually tore her best clothes
or spilled water on her best shoes and slippers
or lost her handkerchief, before she started
for a party. Poor Tess had made up her
mind that nothing was going to happen to
her before she went to Miss Dorothy's
party.

Honey Bunch's mother was not going with them. She had promised to do something for Daddy that afternoon and she had to go downtown. But she waited till the taxicab came and the children went down and climbed into it with Aunt Julia. Dorry told Honey Bunch she looked like a sweet pea.

"Yes'm," he said, "just like a sweet pea. That's the sweetest flower they is, the way I think about it."

Honey Bunch liked riding in the taxicab, but they reached the hotel before she and Tess had found out how to sit in the corner of the leather seat so they would not bounce around. There was a man in uniform to open the taxicab door for them and lift them down. Bobby went on ahead as though he often went to a party in a hotel, but Honey Bunch and Tess kept close to Aunt Julia.

They walked up wide gray stone steps covered with a soft gray carpet and into an elevator that took them upstairs to the floor where Miss Dorothy was giving her party. Bobby went off into one little room and Aunt

Julia and the two little girls were taken into another room.

Such laughing and chattering and running around as there was in this room! There were many mothers and dozens of little girls in the prettiest dresses and with the perkiest hair-ribbons! Some little girls had long curls and some had bobbed straight hair and some had blue eyes and some had brown. But they were all talking at once, so each little girl had the same kind of tongue—that much was certain.

"Now you look very nice and we must go in and speak to Miss Dorothy," said Aunt Julia, when she had made Tess's hair-ribbon stand up and had fixed Honey Bunch's sash so that it would stand out.

They went into a large room with a slippery floor and found Miss Dorothy in the center of more little girls. There were boys, too, as many little boys as girls. Miss Dorothy was a little woman with dark eyes and hair and she smiled at Honey Bunch and said she was very glad to see her.

"Isn't it nice you could come to our party?" said Miss Dorothy. "Tess and Bobby have told me so much about you. Why, I've heard about Honey Bunch ever since I can remember!"

It was a lovely party. Honey Bunch thought it was quite the nicest party she had ever been to. They danced and played games. Bobby showed Honey Bunch how to dance and Kenneth Evans told her how to play the games she did not know. Then when the ice-cream came in—well, no wonder Lester Morris and Bobby had been interested in the ice-cream part of the party, for there were chocolate lions and tigers and vanilla roses and four leaf clovers and plates of the most beautiful little cakes you ever saw. Honey Bunch had a chocolate tiger and Tess had a vanilla rose and Bobby had a lion and Kenneth Evans had a four leaf clover.

Honey Bunch had forgotten about Uncle Paul who liked pink icing till she saw the cakes. Miss Dorothy said that each child should have as many as he liked, but Aunt

Julia told Bobby and Tess that they must not eat more than two, so of course Honey Bunch took only two also. One little cake was covered with pink icing.

"I'm going to save that for Uncle Paul," said Honey Bunch to herself.

She held it in her hand till she had eaten her ice-cream. The waiter came in and took her dish and then, as every one had finished, Miss Dorothy blew her whistle for another game.

"Now I'll go put it in my coat pocket," whispered Honey Bunch, slipping down from her chair and running around behind the empty chairs till she came to the little room where she had left her coat and hat.

No one missed her, for Aunt Julia thought she was playing the game with the others and Bobby and Tess were too excited to know whether she was one of the players or not.

There was no one in the room—the maid had gone to get some of the cake and ice-cream—and Honey Bunch was stuffing her cake into her coat pocket when she looked up and there stood Lester Morris in the doorway.

"Whose coat is that?" he asked, making a face at her.

"It's my coat," said Honey Bunch. "I'm saving something."

"I don't believe a word you say," cried the bad boy, Lester. "That coat belongs to a little girl in this hotel. I'm going to take it back to her!"

Before Honey Bunch knew what he was doing, he had grabbed her coat and darted out into the corridor. Honey Bunch ran after him, but Lester could run faster than she could.

"You're a bad, bad boy!" cried Honey Bunch. "You give me my coat. I'll tell my mother!"

Lester was running so fast that he did not see a man coming toward him. He ran into him and Honey Bunch ran into them both.

"Give me my coat!" she cried, pounding Lester on his back as hard as she could, which wasn't very hard.

"Aren't you ashamed to tease your little sister?" said the man sternly. "Give her the coat at once!"

Without a word Lester handed the coat to Honey Bunch, who was very glad to have it back.

"Now you run along, Sister," said the man kindly. "I'll hold your brother till you are around the corner. I've known boys to be bad again as soon as they thought no one was watching them."

Honey Bunch didn't stop to tell the man that Lester wasn't her brother. Hugging her coat in her arms, she ran, as fast as her little feet could take her, down to the end of the corridor and turned the corner. She kept on running till she had turned another corner. Then she looked back. No Lester was chasing her.

"Somebody," said Honey Bunch, listening a moment, "is talking."

The voice came from a room opposite her. The door was partly open. Honey Bunch pushed it gently and it opened wide enough for her to look in. There were small round

IT WAS A LOVELY PARTY.

Honey Bunch : Her First Visit to the City.   *Page 153*

tables all about the room and men seated at them. One man was standing up and talking. He saw Honey Bunch and stopped. Every one turned and looked at the door. They all saw Honey Bunch.

"Hello!" said the man who had been talking, smiling.

"Hello!" said Honey Bunch, smiling back at him. "Are you having a party, too?"

"It's a party now you've come," said another man, reaching down and lifting her to a table.

CHAPTER XIV

WINTER WEATHER

THE man who had lifted Honey Bunch to the table made her think of her daddy. He took her coat out of her arms and smoothed down her skirts and seemed to know just what to do to make little girls comfortable.

"Sh!" he whispered. "We mustn't talk out loud. Mr. Hubert is going to talk now. Would you like some cake?"

"I had some cake," whispered Honey Bunch. "But I could eat another one. I don't b'lieve Aunt Julia will care."

The man nodded to a waiter who brought Honey Bunch a plate with a slice of white cake on it and a fork to eat it with.

"I'm Mr. Cary," whispered her new friend. "What is your name?"

"Honey Bunch," said the little girl. "What does that mean?"

She leaned forward and touched the silver badge on Mr. Cary's coat. All the men in the room wore silver badges like it.

"That shows I'm a member," explained Mr. Cary, talking in a low tone. "A member of the Hardware Dealers' Association. This is our convention."

Honey Bunch didn't know what a convention was, but she thought it would not be polite to ask any more questions, so she didn't. She ate her cake quietly and listened to Mr. Hubert's speech, though she didn't know what he was talking about. Every one clapped when he sat down.

"I suppose they're glad he's through," said Honey Bunch.

Mr. Cary laughed and the man sitting next to him, who had heard, laughed, too. The party was evidently over, for the men stood up and began to walk around the room. Honey Bunch tried to get down from the table.

"I think I'd better go," she said, and Mr. Cary lifted her down to the floor.

"I'll have to tell Mr. Hubert what you said

about him," he said, still laughing. And before Honey Bunch could say a word, he had shouted across the room, "Oh, Hubert, come over here a minute, will you?"

Mr. Hubert came over and Mr. Cary stood Honey Bunch on a chair and asked her to shake hands.

"Honey Bunch, this is our president, Mr. Hubert," he said, and Honey Bunch shook hands with the man who had made the speech.

Then Mr. Cary whispered something to him, and how Mr. Hubert laughed!

"Were you glad when I had finished speaking, Honey Bunch?" the president asked her, smiling.

"I liked to hear you," said Honey Bunch gravely. "But I didn't know what you were saying. But when I grow up, I will."

"Of course," answered Mr. Hubert, and he took the white flower out of his buttonhole and gave it to her.

Then Honey Bunch said good-bye to Mr. Cary and to the others who asked her to shake

hands with them, and Mr. Cary gave her her
coat and opened the door for her.

"Are you sure you know where to go?" he
asked her, and Honey Bunch said she was sure
she knew.

She went up the corridor and turned
around and before she had gone far she met
Aunt Julia, who was looking for her. All the
way home Honey Bunch told Tess and Bobby
about the "convention" she had seen and
Bobby said that his daddy went to one every
year.

That night it snowed, the first big snowstorm of the winter. No one was more surprised than the children when they woke up
to find the streets covered inches deep with a
white blanket and little white mountains
drifted up against the windows.

"But it wasn't snowing a drop when we went
to bed!" said Honey Bunch.

"Snow likes to surprise us, I think," replied
Uncle Paul. "And this time a whole city has
been caught. I don't believe Bobby and Tess
ought to try to go to school this morning,

Mother," he said to Aunt Julia. "The streets are pretty well filled and they'd have trouble getting through the drifts."

This suited Bobby and Tess exactly. They didn't want to go to school; but they were sure there wasn't one inch too much snow for them to go out and play in. They wanted to go to Maudie Gray's house and play in her back yard.

"If you can walk to Maudie's house, you can certainly get to school," said Aunt Julia firmly. "I don't want you to go out and flounder through the snow until some of the walks are cleaned."

So the children followed Teresa from room to room as she brushed the snow off the window sills with a whisk broom and they stood at the front windows and watched to see if any of the walks were being cleaned. The janitor was shoveling off the pavement before the apartment house and Dorry was helping him.

"Look at Lester Morris!" said Bobby sud-

denly. "Look, he's going to throw a snowball
at Dorry!"

Sure enough, there was Lester, hiding down
beside one of the pine trees and aiming at
Dorry with a large snowball. As the children watched, he threw it, but it missed Dorry
and fell into the gutter.

Lester started to run, but Dorry was too
quick for him. The elevator boy caught him
and paying no attention to Lester's cries, carried him over to the pile of snow he had
shoveled from the steps.

"He's going to wash his face for him!" said
Bobby.

That was exactly what Dorry meant to do,
and he did it thoroughly. When Dorry had
finished scrubbing Lester's face with the
snow, he carried him up the steps and he must
have left him in the hall, for he came down
without him.

"I wish we could go out and make snowballs," sighed Bobby.

"Well, bundle up and run along," Aunt

Julia said. "Take care of Honey Bunch and
don't throw snowballs at any one—remember,
Bobby, not a single ball at any one! Some of
the snow has been cleared away by this time
I am sure."

Mrs. Morton had brought Honey Bunch's
leggings in the trunk and she put them on for
her and brought out her rubbers and a pair of
fuzzy brown mittens instead of the brown
gloves.

"Did you know it would snow, Mother?"
asked Honey Bunch, trying to button her coat
and missing all the buttons because she was so
excited.

"I thought it might," admitted Mrs. Morton. "There now, little daughter, I think
you're cozy. Don't stay out long if you feel
cold."

Bobby and Tess and Honey Bunch walked
down the stairs, for Aunt Julia said the snow
had made extra work for Dorry, and they
must wait on themselves as much as they
could. But Dorry had finished shoveling
snow when they reached the street and they

met him coming up the steps, blowing on his hands to warn them.

"Right cold out," he said cheerfully. "If you want to see the new street cleaners, Bobby, you-all want to walk over to the avenue."

"Let's go over," said Bobby. "It isn't far. Walk fast, Honey Bunch, and you won't be cold."

Honey Bunch wasn't cold. Her cheeks were red, but her fingers and toes were quite warm and cozy. The snow was piled up on each side of the walk, and some places were slippery because all the snow had not been shoveled off.

"Hear the snow plow?" cried Bobby as they neared the avenue. "Look out, Honey Bunch —don't let it blow in your eyes!"

The great snow plow was running up and down the trolley tracks, clearing the snow away. It was a machine with the largest and stiffest brush Honey Bunch had ever seen— the scrubbing brush Mrs. Miller used was never half as stiff as this brush. It made the snow fly in clouds, and if you didn't stand well

back on the sidewalk and close your eyes when
it went past, some of the snow was pretty sure
to blow in them.

"The wagons are working, too," said
Bobby, pointing to a line of horses and wagons
standing in the deep snow. "The men shovel
off that snow, Honey Bunch, and take it
away."

"Where?" asked Honey Bunch.

She thought perhaps they took the snow
somewhere for children to play in and build
snow forts and snow men. But no, Bobby said,
the snow was taken off and dumped in the
river.

"They have to get it out of the way," he explained. "Daddy told me. If it stayed in the
streets, another snowstorm might come and
then another one and by and by no milk wagons could bring us milk and no cars could run
and we might starve."

"Come on and let's run on top of the snow
banks," said Tess, who didn't like to stand
still and look at anything long, no matter how

interesting it might be. "The snow's packed hard enough, Bobby, let's climb up."

Running along the top of the snow banks was exciting, and Honey Bunch fell off only once. That didn't hurt her, for she fell in the soft snow, but when Tess fell off and hit her knee on the curbstone, she decided that she had played long enough in the snow and wanted to go home.

When Mr. Turner came home to dinner that night he said it was much colder out. He said there would surely be skating.

"Can't we take Honey Bunch to Central Park and let her see the lake?" asked Tess, whose knee had stopped hurting as soon as she was in the warm house.

"And she hasn't seen the monkeys," added Bobby. "I think she ought to see the monkeys, Mother."

His mother laughed and so did Mrs. Morton. Honey Bunch did not laugh. She was busy remembering that Kitty Williams had asked her to bring home a little monkey if they gave them away in New York. Perhaps she could get a little monkey in Central Park. She would ask Tess about it before she went to bed.

"I suppose Central Park is a place Honey Bunch must see," said Bobby's mother. "I can not go with you to-morow, but I think your Aunt Edith will. She and Honey Bunch can meet you at the Park to-morrow after school. You won't have to come home, and that will give you a nice, long afternoon."

So Honey Bunch and her mother went to Central Park the next afternoon to meet Bobby and Tess. There was enough snow for all the children in the world—at least Honey Bunch thought there was—in Central Park. It was very white and beautiful and no one had walked on it, except where the walks had been cleared off.

"Isn't it cold!" cried Tess, running up to them. "Let's go in the monkey house first and get warm. Bobby and I nearly froze walking in."

Honey Bunch had remembered to ask Tess

about the little monkey as they were getting
ready for bed and Tess had told her that she
was sure no monkeys were ever given away.

"Anyway," said Tess sensibly, "you wait till
you see the monkeys and then you'll know that
you couldn't carry one back to Barham.
Monkeys won't keep still a minute. I guess,"
added Tess, "that is why Daddy calls me a
monkey."

But even Tess couldn't wriggle and squirm
and climb and chatter as constantly as those
monkeys did. Honey Bunch stood and stared
at them as they twisted and jumped about in
the cages. There was one cunning little one
that would have been nice for Kitty, but
Honey Bunch knew as soon as she saw him
that he wouldn't be good on the train. He
was the kind of monkey who couldn't keep out
of mischief. He was teasing another monkey
even then.

"It is cute, but I guess I couldn't get it
home to Kitty, even if the man gave it to me,"
said Honey Bunch. "What do you think
Bobby?"

"You could not!" was Bobby's very decided answer.

"Now let's go down to the lake," said Tess. "I'm all warm, aren't you? Are you warm, Aunt Edith?"

Honey Bunch's mother said she was quite warm and they started to walk down to the lake. A cold wind blew in their faces, but the skaters didn't seem to mind the wind. The lake was filled and they were darting back and forth and making circles and fancy figures, and of course they wouldn't be cold when they were having such an interesting time.

CHAPTER XV

A GRAND SURPRISE

"We can walk on the edge of the ice," said Bobby, "Come on—I'll hold your hand, Honey Bunch, and you can slide."

"Don't go out too far," said Honey Bunch's mother. "Some of the skaters might skate into you, Bobby."

"We'll be careful," promised Bobby. "Tess, want to slide? You can hang on to my belt."

Tess took hold of the belt of her brother's overcoat and Honey Bunch took his hand and Mrs. Morton waved to them as they started slowly to slide.

"This ice," said Honey Bunch, as she almost fell down, "is very slippery, isn't it?"

"Central Park ice is always slippery," boasted Bobby. "I guess more people fall down on this lake than anywhere else."

Honey Bunch kept on sliding, but her hands were cold and by and by her feet didn't feel right, either.

"I can't feel my feet when I walk on them, Bobby," she explained.

"You're cold," said Bobby, looking at his little cousin and noticing how red her small nose was. "Your feet are cold, too. I tell you what we'll do; we'll go up in the house and get warm. Tess will go and tell Aunt Edith, won't you, Tess? Tell her Honey Bunch was cold and I took her up to the house to let her get warm. We'll meet you over by the elephants."

"The house" Bobby spoke of was a building where the skaters went to thaw out when they were too cold to skate another step. There was a fire and many people were walking up and down the room, stamping to warm their cold feet. Honey Bunch stamped, too.

She was just going to ask Bobby if she could go up to the fire and hold her hands out to the blaze when suddenly some one outside shouted and every one began to run for the door.

"Some one fell in!" shouted a boy, pulling open the door. "Gee, I'll bet he drowns!"

"I'll be right back! You stay here!" said Bobby to Honey Bunch, and away he ran with the others.

Honey Bunch was left all alone. She walked over to the fire and warmed her hands, then she looked out of each window, and still Bobby didn't come back! By standing on one of the seats she could see the crowd around the lake.

"I hope no one drowns," said Honey Bunch aloud. "It must take a large hole to fall through the ice."

She meant that it must take a large hole to let a person fall through the ice. Honey Bunch did not know that sometimes the ice is much thinner in one place than in another and that a skater may skate right through and land in the icy water before he knows it.

"I'll go find Bobby," said Honey Bunch, when several more minutes had gone and no Bobby came.

She pulled back the heavy door—and she

had to use both hands to do it—and stepped out into the snow. She looked down the hill to the lake, but she couldn't see any black and red checked cap like the one Bobby wore.

"I think I'll go down this path," decided Honey Bunch. "Maybe I'll meet Bobby coming up."

Honey Bunch didn't like the idea of trying to find Bobby in the crowd around the lake. She was the least little bit shy of many strange people and she hoped her cousin would find her before she had to ask any one where he was. But though the path she was following turned and twisted and went around behind bushes and out again, she didn't meet Bobby on it.

"That looks like the monkey house!" said Honey Bunch in surprise, when she found herself standing in front of a building she thought she remembered.

It was the monkey house, and Honey Bunch went in. Perhaps Bobby had stopped to look again at the monkeys. Instead of Bobby, the first person she saw was Lester Morris!

"Hello!" he said to her. "Where did you come from?"

"I'm looking for Bobby," replied Honey Bunch politely. "Have you seen him?"

"Did you and Bobby come all alone to the Park?" asked Lester, holding a peanut out to a monkey and pulling it back as the animal grabbed for it.

"No, Mother and Tess and Bobby and I came," explained Honey Bunch. "Bobby and I went to get warm, and then he ran out to see who was drowned and he hasn't come back yet."

"He won't come back," said Lester, shelling another peanut. "I saw him going home. Your mother and Tess, too. They said they were tired and they thought they'd go home and rest."

Honey Bunch stared at him.

"But—but I'm here!" she said. "They wouldn't go home and leave me."

"Huh, wouldn't they?" Lester said disagreeably. "You might as well make up your mind not to see any of your folks again. Lots

of people leave their children in the monkey
house and the keeper puts 'm in cages and
after a while you'd never know them from the
monkeys."

Poor Honey Bunch! She didn't know
whether to believe Lester or not. He seemed
to be telling the truth, but surely Mother
wouldn't go home and leave her little girl
alone in Central Park. And her daddy
wouldn't like it at all if she were put in a cage
like a monkey!

"This monkey was a little girl once," said
Lester, who was as bad as he could be, and
that was pretty bad, you may have guessed.
Lester told the biggest fibs and none of his
friends could ever believe him. If Honey
Bunch had only known him a little longer, she
would have known at once that he wasn't telling a word of truth.

"Yes, sir, this monkey's name was Gladys,"
said Lester, holding out a peanut and then
putting it in his own mouth as the monkey
tried to take it.

Honey Bunch stared at him while he

shelled another peanut. Her eyes were so full
of tears that she didn't see him hold it out to
the monkey, but she heard him scream.

"Ow! He's killing me! Come quick,
somebody, the monkey is killing me!"
screamed Lester.

He had gone too close to the cage and the
monkey had grabbed his ear and was pulling
it almost as hard as Lester sometimes pulled
the tails of the monkeys.

Honey Bunch saw the keeper come running
and the monkey saw him, too. He let go of
Lester's ear and jumped to the top of the cage
where he sat chattering with rage and telling
every monkey in the house what he thought of
such a bad boy.

Lester started to run as soon as the monkey
let go his ear, and he was in such a hurry to
get away that he never watched where he was
going, but tumbled, Plop! into a tub of water
by the door.

"And right it serves you!" scolded the
keeper, fishing him out. "This isn't the first
time I've seen you teasing the monkeys. If I

had caught you first I should have warmed
your jacket for you. If I ever see you teasing
one of the monkeys again, I'm going to send
for a policeman and let him take care of you."

A number of people had gathered around,
for they had heard Lester screaming. One of
the men offered now to take the boy up to the
engine room and dry him off and the keeper
said that it was much too good for him.

"Still, he looks cold now and I wouldn't be
wishing my worst enemy a fit of sickness,"
went on the keeper, frowning at Lester, whose
teeth were chattering like the monkey's, although Lester's teeth chattered because the
water into which he had fallen was ice-cold.
"Take him out of my sight, do, and while
you're drying him off, teach him some
manners."

The man took Lester away and Honey
Bunch stepped up and pulled the keeper's
coat sleeve.

"Please," she said, "where do you keep lost
folks in this park?"

"Are you lost?" asked the keeper, smiling

until you wouldn't think he was the same man who had scolded Lester.

"No—o, I'm not lost," declared Honey Bunch. "But Bobby is. And my mother and Tess. They won't know where—why, here they are! That's Mother!"

Honey Bunch had seen Bobby coming through the door and her mother and Tess following him.

"I told you we'd find her here!" cried Tess, as Honey Bunch ducked under an old gentleman's cane and jumped straight into her mother's arms. "I *knew* she'd gone back to see the monkeys."

Well, the keeper and every one else who had heard Honey Bunch ask about her lost people were very glad that they had all found each other. Bobby said it was really Honey Bunch's fault because she hadn't stayed where he had told her to stay. No one had been drowned, after all, and as soon as he had found that out he had hurried back.

"Another time, Bobby, don't leave a little girl, even to find out what is happening somewhere else," said Mrs. Morton gravely. "When you are taking care of a girl in a crowd, you mustn't leave her to look after herself. But when you are a little older, dear, you'll understand this better."

As they had all had enough of the ice that day, they went to see the elephants and Honey Bunch thought they were as large as Uncle Paul's office building.

"Well, they're almost as tall," she argued, when Bobby laughed and said an elephant wasn't so tall if you didn't think so.

Honey Bunch liked the squirrels, too, and so did Tess.

"Stub says she can see squirrels any day," said Tess. "I suppose they like to live in the country."

"Yes, squirrels do live in the woods," answered Mrs. Morton. "And if Honey Bunch goes to visit Stub this summer, she will see these same kind of pretty squirrels, but living happily outdoors. You would like that, wouldn't you, dear?"

Honey Bunch thought she would like it

very much. Her cousin Mary, whom they all called "Stub," lived on a farm and Honey Bunch had never seen a farm. Whether she did see squirrels living in the woods and what she and Stub found to do the summer weeks they spent together, must be left for another book. You'll find Honey Bunch's farm adventures in the story called "Honey Bunch: Her First Days on the Farm."

Going home from Central Park, Honey Bunch found a great surprise waiting for her. Bobby and Tess were surprised, too, but Honey Bunch's mother and her Aunt Julia and Uncle Paul did not seem to feel surprised.

"You-all have company," Dorry said, smiling, as he took them up in the elevator.

Honey Bunch went in first. There sat a gentleman, talking to her Uncle Paul.

"Daddy!" cried Honey Bunch. "Oh, Daddy, when did you come? Mother, here's Daddy!"

And Daddy Morton kissed Honey Bunch and her mother at the same time and asked them if they were ready to go home with him.

"All right—let's," said Honey Bunch. "I would like to see Lady Clare."

But they couldn't go that night, of course, and Daddy Morton stayed in New York several days. Then they went back to Barham and Honey Bunch found that home was a pretty nice place. She thought she would never want to go away again, but she did. The very next summer she went to see Stub. So, you see, little girls sometimes change their minds.

THE END

THE MAKE-BELIEVE STORIES

(Trademark Registered.)

By LAURA LEE HOPE

Author of THE BOBBSEY TWINS BOOKS, ETC.

Colored Wrappers and Illustrations by HARRY L. SMITH

In this fascinating line of books Miss Hope has the various toys come to life "when nobody is looking" and she puts them through a series of adventures as interesting as can possibly be imagined.

THE STORY OF A SAWDUST DOLL

How the toys held a party at the Toy Counter; how the Sawdust Doll was taken to the home of a nice little girl, and what happened to her there.

THE STORY OF A WHITE ROCKING HORSE

He was a bold charger and a man purchased him for his son's birthday. Once the Horse had to go to the Toy Hospital, and my! what sights he saw there.

THE STORY OF A LAMB ON WHEELS

She was a dainty creature and a sailor bought her and took her to a little girl relative and she had a great time.

THE STORY OF A BOLD TIN SOLDIER

He was Captain of the Company and marched up and down in the store at night. Then he went to live with a little boy and had the time of his life.

THE STORY OF A CANDY RABBIT

He was continually in danger of losing his life by being eaten up. But he had plenty of fun, and often saw his many friends from the Toy Counter.

THE STORY OF A MONKEY ON A STICK

He was mighty lively and could do many tricks. The boy who owned him gave a show, and many of the Monkey's friends were among the actors.

THE STORY OF A CALICO CLOWN

He was a truly comical chap and all the other toys loved him greatly.

THE STORY OF A NODDING DONKEY

He made happy the life of a little lame boy and did lots of other good deeds.

THE STORY OF A CHINA CAT

The China Cat had many adventures, but enjoyed herself most of the time.

THE STORY OF A PLUSH BEAR

This fellow came from the North Pole, stopped for a while at the toy store, and was then taken to the seashore by his little master.

THE STORY OF A STUFFED ELEPHANT

He was a wise looking animal and had a great variety of adventures.

GROSSET & DUNLAP,   PUBLISHERS,   NEW YORK

THE BOBBSEY TWINS BOOKS

For Little Men and Women
By LAURA LEE HOPE
Author of "The Bunny Brown" Series, Etc.

12mo. DURABLY BOUND. ILLUSTRATED. UNIFORM STYLE OF BINDING

Copyright publications which cannot be obtained elsewhere. Books that charm the hearts of the little ones, and of which they never tire.

THE BOBBSEY TWINS

THE BOBBSEY TWINS IN THE COUNTRY

THE BOBBSEY TWINS AT THE SEASHORE

THE BOBBSEY TWINS AT SCHOOL

THE BOBBSEY TWINS AT SNOW LODGE

THE BOBBSEY TWINS ON A HOUSEBOAT

THE BOBBSEY TWINS AT MEADOW BROOK

THE BOBBSEY TWINS AT HOME

THE BOBBSEY TWINS IN A GREAT CITY

THE BOBBSEY TWINS ON BLUEBERRY ISLAND

THE BOBBSEY TWINS ON THE DEEP BLUE SEA

THE BOBBSEY TWINS IN THE GREAT WEST

GROSSET & DUNLAP,   PUBLISHERS,   NEW YORK

SIX LITTLE BUNKERS SERIES

By LAURA LEE HOPE

Author of "The Bobbsey Twins Books,"
"The Bunny Brown Series,"
"The Make-Believe Series," Etc.

Durably Bound. Illustrated. Uniform Style of Binding

Delightful stories for little boys and girls which sprung into immediate popularity. To know the six little Bunkers is to take them at once to your heart, they are so intensely human, so full of fun and cute sayings. Each story has a little plot of its own——one that can be easily followed——and all are written in Miss Hope's most entertaining manner. Clean, wholesome volumes which ought to be on the bookshelf of every child in the land.

SIX LITTLE BUNKERS AT GRANDMA BELL'S
SIX LITTLE BUNKERS AT AUNT JO'S
SIX LITTLE BUNKERS AT COUSIN TOM'S
SIX LITTLE BUNKERS AT GRANDPA FORDS
SIX LITTLE BUNKERS AT UNCLE FRED'S
SIX LITTLE BUNKERS AT CAPTAIN BEN'S
SIX LITTLE BUNKERS AT COWBOY JACK'S

GROSSET & DUNLAP,   PUBLISHERS,   NEW YORK

THE OUTDOOR GIRLS SERIES
By LAURA LEE HOPE
Author of the popular "Bobbsey Twin Books" and "Bunny Brown" Series.

UNIFORM STYLE OF BINDING.   INDIVIDUAL COLORED WRAPPERS.

These tales take in the various adventures participated in by several bright, up-to-date girls who love outdoor life. They are clean and wholesome, free from sensationalism, and absorbing from the first chapter to the last.

THE OUTDOOR GIRLS OF DEEPDALE
Or Camping and Tramping for Fun and Health.

THE OUTDOOR GIRLS AT RAINBOW LAKE
Or Stirring Cruise of the Motor Boat Gem.

THE OUTDOOR GIRLS IN A MOTOR CAR
Or The Haunted Mansion of Shadow Valley.

THE OUTDOOR GIRLS IN A WINTER CAMP
Or Glorious Days on Skates and Ice Boats.

THE OUTDOOR GIRLS IN FLORIDA
Or Wintering in the Sunny South.

THE OUTDOOR GIRLS AT OCEAN VIEW
Or The Box that Was Found in the Sand.

THE OUTDOOR GIRLS ON PINE ISLAND
Or A Cave and What it Contained.

THE OUTDOOR GIRLS IN ARMY SERVICE
Or Doing Their Bit for Uncle Sam.

THE OUTDOOR GIRLS AT THE HOSTESS
HOUSE
Or Doing Their Best for the Soldiers.

THE OUTDOOR GIRLS AT BLUFF POINT
Or A Wreck and A Rescue.

THE OUTDOOR GIRLS AT WILD ROSE LODGE
Or The Hermit of Moonlight Falls.

THE OUTDOOR GIRLS IN THE SADDLE
Or The Girl Miner of Gold Run.

GROSSET & DUNLAP,   PUBLISHERS,   NEW YORK